Engaging The Dragon

Engaging The Dragon

Kenna McKinnon

Chapter One

Almere felt the dragon's bulk sizzle between her thighs, hard and smooth like riding a man. How she missed her husband, Stannock, far away at the wars in the northwest!

She and her dragon dropped through shouting halls of air, wheeled dead-stop before the cliff that led to her father-in-law's castle, then Fire-Smasher banked and rose, blazing, to the top of the wall.

"Hello, the guard below! Almere demands the right to enter." She pulled on the rein of fire that controlled her pet, her blue eyes sparkling in a tan face. Her yellow wide-brimmed hat flapped in the breeze created by the descending dragon.

"Open the landing roofs and make way for the princess," the guards called.

Armor clinked below. Soldiers leaned on the great chains that supported the roof gates which slowly ground apart.

Once in the King's castle, her dragon pranced high above on wings of translucent emerald, scarlet, and periwinkle blue. Almere forced a cooler breath to calm the flutter in her chest.

"You weren't gone long this time." Stannock's half-brother leaned against a pillar. The portico yawned in the open air, inviting rest. "The dragon is fed?"

"Suitable shrubs and rodents from the valley." Almere slumped into an expanse of pillows within the queen's chair. The Queen mother rode a beast of her own under the burning triple suns of the planet Draxxt and seldom came home before nightfall.

The Queen's dragons were not like Fire-Smasher. All of the other dragons were faster and stronger – fierce and waiting for a battle. Fire-Smasher, whom Almere rode astride, fast and desperate before her husband left for the wars – "Kiss me, Stannock, kiss me hard," she begged and her wet mouth clung to his, two of their four full moons ago. Now there was his brother, sturdy and insolent, who stared at her with moist dark eyes half hidden under drooping lids.

"Almere."

"Where is the Queen?" she asked.

"She plays the part of a young girl, as usual, up and away in the clouds until the last sun's set." Tevron moved only his lips, then the tips of his fingers wriggled in his tight pockets. The pillar supported his weight. His body shifted to stand more firmly on his feet. Almere feared he would lunge in her direction, and what would she do then? A face like her husband's but darker and older on his bold smiling half-brother, his bodyguard and rival, the brother who stayed behind as king's advisor while Stannock fought on the fronts of the wars. All these months, her husband was gone, her bed empty.

Almere twisted a piece of her wavy black hair in her fingers, blue eyes flashing.

"I must bathe, Tevron," she said. She was able to mask her fear from him; with a dismissive gesture, she got to her feet.

Tevron nodded but he was not ready for her to leave. "Mariette will run your bath. The servants have heated the water already."

"It's good of the queen's maids to wait on me so."

"Only fitting for the queen's daughter-in-law. What do you know from the day's trip?"

She stretched and her muscles welcomed the release of tension. She could feel his hard stare on her half naked body, her bodice pulled apart from the fierce ride. "It's been a hard ride, and the spies in the northwest have come back with no news. I saw the fires at the edge of Gracklen. I'm afraid for Stannock."

"Afraid for my brother and his soldiers?" The thick figure in the shade of the portico moved into the light of a double moon. Night came suddenly in Gracklen. "They fight for the land of the Trolls at Many Waters. It's all about land. There is another solution than war, but my brother is thick-headed and won't listen. Though he's brave, I'll give him that."

Her loins ached.

"Damn him," she cursed.

"You miss him?" Tevron stalked like a dark animal to her side.

Out of annoyance, Almere flicked the dragon whip still in her hand. "That is not a question."

"I know you, Almere. I've seen the desire in your eyes, felt your heart smolder like hot coals."

She drew back and thought of her husband, so different from his dark brother, and she felt afraid again. She could see Tevron's thin white smile in the gloaming.

"He's sent no word of the war. The dragons here are restless to join their cousins and flock," Tevron said. "My own beast has long since been lost in the wars, flown to accompany Stannock with his servant and baggage, my mount torn from me because I chose to stay at the palace and attend the King. That's all right. Dragons are scarce. I have my eye on a young one, eager to grow and learn from its master." He smirked at the thought of a new pet.

"You will never mount my Fire-Smasher," Almere denied, aware of his designs. "You wait here, Tevron, and torment me while you let your brother go to war on your behalf."

"My mother, the Queen, wishes for grandchildren, while you remain barren due to my absent brother. Didn't I take the better path? If you would allow it, I would step in for my brother. Stannock is useless here, but active on the front where he fights instead of loves."

The Queen wished for grandchildren, and Almere was alone here without a husband to spawn them. If only she could produce heirs. Queen Ericaania reminded her often of her barrenness. Almere had no other husband. Not like Ericaania, who took two husbands and then was left with only the old King, Hakor, who had murdered the Queen's first love and left her with their strange dark child, Tevron. Almere knew that her mother-in-law never forgave King Hakor, but from that day on, she feared the king's displeasure because of the bargain she had struck to keep her and the dead Malcoom's child alive and under King Hakor's protection.

Tevron slipped his hand under the silky fabric of Almere's bodice. "I have no wish to be murdered at a meal or in bed," he assured her. "I can wait."

She flicked her whip onto the back of his hand and screwed her mouth downwards. Her stomach heaved. "I have no wish to sleep with you."

A dragon looped through the evening sky, talons outstretched to alight on a high tower.

"I AM DESTRUCTION," the dragon gloated. "I AM FATE." It smiled and settled on the tower, guided by reins of fire held in the hand of a tanned, older but supple woman.

"Ericaania has returned."

"My cue to depart," Tevron said and left. His voice so much like her husband's, away at a war they may not win, a war Almere longed to rejoin with her dragon and his friends, Queen Ericaania in the lead with sure hands on the flaming reins of her plunging mount.

Fire-Smasher, Almere's immature red dragon, leaped in a stream of fire to be with the larger dragon. The King's guards grasped the sparkling reins that hung from above and led both dragons to their stables for the night where they were free to eat small live mammals and count their gold. The Queen's dragon, a translucent crimson flame in the dark, slipped from the top of the tower to the landing platform near the Great Hall, then his great low voice hummed from within the castle stronghold. Almere heard Fire-Smasher reply with a low hiss. He attempted to prophecy the battle tomorrow. Almere felt her loins weaken and she moistened.

"Is the King not glad to see me?" Ericaania's words came from deep within a cave of fire, her dragon flickering in the night from the stables below.

The King's reply rumbled from the Great Hall. Guards came out to secure the inner gates. Two moons rose high in a night black and as sticky as Almere's own sweat.

"I was delayed by a happy feast in our neighbor's garden," Almere could hear her mother-in-law say. "I thought of my lord the entire time, and we got away as soon as we could, my dragon Lockjaw and I."

The King's voice rumbled in reply.

"Did you have a good time today, Mother?" Almere stood inside the barred doors and faced the woman she might have loved, given other circumstances. "Did our neighbors treat you well at the feast? As they always must, for you're always late at this time of year, coming from their hospitality. When the early cold comes on us during the evening, and it's only at home that we're comfortable. We miss you, Mother, the King especially."

"Yes," the Queen replied. She put her arms around Almere, who pulled away uncomfortably. "Now a hug and off to your bath you go. First you, then me, for I'm chilled to the liver with the long ride today."

"Long ride? What about the feast with the neighbors?" Almere reminded her, eyes misted, sorry for the King. "Mother, I'm sick about your lies. Father doesn't deserve this, and neither do I."

"Lies? You sorry skinny bag of fluff." The Queen laughed. "You're just like I used to be at your age, Almere. A papa's girl. If your own father had lived, and your mother hadn't been banished at such a young age, you might have grown to be a proper wife."

"But I had my father's dowry," Almere reminded her. "And he loved the King, your husband. Enough to betroth me to the King's only son at a young age, before we were of age to consent."

"Should have been someone else," Ericaania complained. "You are barren, child."

"Not enough time to decide that yet," defended the younger woman. "And how do you know it is me?" she asked boldly, not considering the wrath of the Queen at such an impertinent suggestion.

"Our son will provide us with an heir yet," the Queen declared confidently. "Either with you or he'll take another wife."

Almere's heart trembled and her gut twisted. It was possible Stannock would take another wife, she knew that. They had tried for an heir for ten cycles of the moons already, and she was still as slim and barren as when she had come as a virgin bride to his bed.

The King rumbled a few more words from within his room next to the Great Hall. Almere stood in the foyer with Ericaania and listened to the sick man cough.

"Coming, dear." Ericaania's voice echoed through the tapestry-lined rooms. "I'll wheel you out to say goodnight to Almere."

"If I could move, I'd wheel *myself* out there and shoot you through the eyes." The King raised his voice to cover the sound of weeping. Who was weeping? Not her mother-in-law — it was the King, and Almere bowed her head in sympathy. The Great Hall was not so great that sound couldn't travel through the tiled and tapestried hallways to the foyer where she stood. The King cried out, and the wheels of his chair scraped against the doorway as his massive torso lunged past the smoking torches on the walls to greet his beloved daughter-in-law, whom he cherished as his own flesh. The Queen stood in the background, forgotten. Her jaw was set.

Fire-Smasher and Lockjaw, their meals finished, circled overhead, now crimson transparent in the light of the double moons. The other two moons were rising. Almere could clearly see the outline of her husband's older brother leaning against the balustrades outside, half hidden by dark shrubs, his face sullen and his eyes smoldering as he glared into the porticos of the Great Hall. She could feel the man's lust and hatred burning into her heart even with the distance between them. Almere shuddered, put her cool arms around the warm body of King Hakor, and joined the Queen in the depths of the palace. There was a sound in the night, close by, a rattle and thud, and then all lay silent beneath the moonlight streaming through the window slits of the inner chambers, surrounded by green silk, embroidered tapestries, great bronze shields, and blood-encrusted pikes.

Almere stopped to pick up the large red stone thrown through the portico above. "It's a sign," Ericaania said. "The rabble are out there, waiting to get us."

"We're not safe," Almere agreed, smoothing her thumb along the pebbled, ruddy surface. "This is enough to have crushed my head if it had found its mark." She knew, though, that the stone had not been thrown by a peasant nor an unhappy servant. Someone lurked in the shadows outside, who hated her and the Palace and the Court. Someone very close to home – and dangerous.

She shuddered. *Come home, Stannock. I need no protector but you, and my dragon speaks of deception. Come home and share my bed. I need you, my husband. Let your Captain take care of the battle in your absence. Captain Devvid and the old general are well able to do so.*

There was never any answer to the prayers she sent to the skies. Her marriage bed remained cold and bleak. Cold like the beating heart of her husband's brother and his lustful eyes which taunted her with their crippled resemblance to Stannock's, or a mockery of the twin jewels of Fire-Smasher's orbs, burning with a patient desire. She thought of the old prophecy of a Dracaena or half human, half dragon female who would save the land of Draxxt. If the bloodline were to come through the Royal lineage, as the legend intimated, she didn't know how or from where it would spring. Perhaps the Palace was haunted and perhaps she was cursed.

Chapter Two

Tevron glared at the profile of his sister-in-law outlined by the flickering flames in the foyer of the Great Hall. Tevron's half- brother, Stannock, was second in command of the army that fought in northwestern Gracklen, their country, a war with the invading Trolls and colorful Picts far beyond the borders of the King's castle and the crippled King himself.

"My brother is a brave man and foolish, as brave men are, more heart than brains," Tevron muttered to his servant. He continued to cast glances at the slim young woman beyond the courtyard as a plan took shape in his hot brain. He wore tight black trousers and a silver coat, open at the chest, where dark hairs curled luxuriously about a metallic swastika icon on a sturdy chain. The servant Paige stood next to him, a willowy wraith by an oak tree, the servant's adolescent body still unformed and gangly, hair blond and curly, grey eyes fixed on his master.

Almere was not aware when Tevron stopped his scrutiny and turned his back on the palace. His own living quarters were humbler and this irked his molten soul – he, the son allowed to live, of a former king murdered by his rival, the still young King Hakor. He was only half-brother to Stannock, who was the favored son and sole male legitimate heir.

Tevron bent and picked up a sizable red stone, muttered an incantation over it, and pitched it at a flickering window slit of the palace. His mother had begged King Hakor for Tevron's life and he had granted it in exchange for silence about Malcoom's death. That silence had cost her dearly through the years, for she had loved Malcoom more than Hakor, and her knowledge might have been a means of controlling her second husband if it were not for her dark son and the need to protect him. For Ericaania was ambitious and thwarted in that ambition, and thus the long wild rides during the day, and the lovers, he thought.

"May it bring you a curse," Tevron muttered as the stone took flight, and Paige beside him grinned. They heard the distant thud as the stone ricocheted off the portico and into the inner hall.

"I'm sure it will, sir. It will at least make her consider the source, for a moment, and perhaps fear." The young man slapped his hand on his thigh. "Tis cold," he complained. "I'll draw you a hot bath and warm your sheets with hot bricks."

"Damn you." Tevron drew a flask from a pouch at the waistband of his tight black pants and drank deeply. He wiped his mouth with the back of a dirty fist and replaced the flask in the pouch.

"Sir?" Paige stood a head shorter than Tevron; he looked up to inquire of his master.

"Yes, a hot bath. And damn them all to Hades."

"Sir?"

"The women control the old king, my father Malcoom's rival. Why did Hakor let me live?

A wolf would have destroyed his enemy's children. He's a weakling, and he'll live to regret it."

"The walls have ears," Paige whispered in earnest.

"Yes, and it's high treason I speak of, my words flow foolishly with anger and ale. We'll see my brother dead and the old king put out of his misery before the winter's on us, my brother's young widow in my bed, and my mother banished. With her coterie of dragon shit."

Paige led the way to the sumptuous rooms at the end of the portico. "They say the dragons are enchanted. They can talk, and they know the future."

Tevron scratched his crotch. "They love fresh meat, gold, and their riders, but I'll lure them away. I'll have an army of my own, with my faithful followers and the Palace guards that even now hide in the shadows." He threw aside the heavy curtains just inside his doorway.

Almere threw her cloak over her shoulder and strode into the women's quarters where the maid Mariette had filled a large soaking tub with hot water, lavender, and soap. Thick white towels and rose-scented lotions lined a rack near the lip of the tub. Almere slipped off her riding trousers and rough crimson blouse, dropped her undergarments on the floor, and sank to her neck in the steaming liquid.

"Ahhhhh. Dragon's breath, this is heaven."

Her toes projected from the bubbles and she wiggled them, then began to cleanse herself with a hunk of creamy soap half again as large as her hand. She splashed scented water on her face and scrubbed off the oil and dirt from the long ride home on Fire-Smasher. Over mountains blue with snow and valleys hot with dust they had soared, scouring the land for signs of Trolls or painted Picts or perhaps for returning Gracklen warriors, defeated at last in battle. She saw no sign of her princely husband or his troop of men and women.

That's a good omen. He must be all right; no imperial dragon was seen carrying my husband's body home today or in the last four moon cycles.

She moved the soapy lather down her body to her firm young breasts and circled the pink rosebuds at the tips. Steam rose from her body and the tub enveloped her completely as she sank further into its watery womb, up to her chin. The soap slipped from her fingertips and she touched that private part which only three others had so far breached – the earnest young student in middle school, fumbling with her buttons in the classroom left empty and echoing of all but their hot young bodies, exploring, eager…his lips on her neck. She remembered their outraged teacher who discovered them when coming back for a forgotten book, their outraged parents when told, her father's nod and knowing smile, the smack of her mother's hand on her cheek – then the riding lessons and the handsome young instructor for a short, hot summer – then Stannock and consummation of a favored royal marriage for which she had saved her final virginity. As her fingers slipped into that secret place, probing, rubbing, a ragged breath tore through her body, the pubic hair curling beneath her hand. The tub steamed, the air hung grey with mist and desire, lavender and rose petals competed with the smell of musk. She glanced up and saw Mariette watching her from the doorway.

"It's Tevron," Mariette explained her interruption. "He has a message from the King for Prince Stannock's commanding officer."

How long has she been standing there?

Almere caught her breath and rose, dripping, from the tub. Mariette moved swiftly and pulled a thick white towel over the girl's nakedness.

"You'll catch your death of cold, honey." Mariette's voice sounded dry. "You want to be presentable enough to meet the Queen tonight. She called for you earlier." Practiced hands moved the towel over Almere's bare body. She was tempted to direct the maid's hands to that secret place, but thought better of it, shrugged on a fuzzy robe, and looked around for her maids who would escort her to the Queen's chambers.

Tevron appeared instead, as though he had been standing outside the door. His dark hair was wet and plastered back from his recently scrubbed face. Paige hovered in the background. Almere pulled back her square shoulders and suggested it was best not to disturb the Queen further that night. Her bath had taken longer than usual, and the Queen's windows were dark.

"The King has given me a message for Stannock's general, to be delivered tomorrow – at first dawn, we must follow the men's march to the northwest and deliver it into the general's hands and no other. Even I don't know what's in the message," Tevron lied. Paige shuffled his feet and looked at the floor tiles.

"Paige will leave at sunrise with the message, and he'll need a dragon."

He would take Fire-Smasher, the immature red dragon, because they couldn't spare another.

Almere's legs trembled. The letter was sealed with the King's gold wax, stamped with his royal ring, and no one in the kingdom except the general would dare to open it now.

Not even me.

As soon as Tevron strode away, with the message tucked into a pouch at his waist, she lowered herself onto the couch in the sitting room next to the women's quarters. *Pray God, is it good news? Is the King recalling my dear husband back to my loving arms?*

"I'll help you pack, Paige," Tevron offered to his servant. "Be careful with the dragon. He's untried with a male rider and a strong arm, other than that girl my brother married."

"I'm an excellent rider, sir," the servant replied. "The message will get through or I'll die trying."

Tevron pulled on his lip. "Just so." He poured a glass of his best dark ale, holding it to his nostrils for a moment to savor the hoppy smell, then slapped his servant on the back. "I do hope no one has to…"

Paige folded a small riding blanket into his rucksack. "What's that, sir?"

"…die trying," Tevron finished. He smiled, showing many square white teeth, sharp in his tanned face, like a fighting dog.

Chapter Three

Fire-Smasher, the smallest dragon, hatched only ten months ago, born from the union of Lock-jaw and Faerydust. As dragons will, he grew with astonishing speed and was trained to the fiery rein about the same time Stannock left the high mountain castle for the wars. Lock-jaw was very vocal and trained the little dragon well in nuances of epic poetry, prophecy, and battle phrases. Because of his unique coloring, the trainers called him Fire-Smasher, but his scales would glow purple, blue, and green when the sweet creature sailed in front of a sun or grew alarmed or excited. Because of his youth, he was a poor choice for anyone to ride to the battles in the northwest, but unfortunately, the war had taken most of the good mounts from the King's castle to use in action. The Picts and

Trolls howled and fought against their monarch in the furthest reaches of the King's lands. Paige was but a boy, and light, so the most likely rider for the smallest dragon.

Tevron folded the sealed royal letter into his servant's saddlebag the night before, cautioning him to say nothing of his precious cargo other than what Almere knew, and to deliver it directly to Stannock's commanding officer in camp without stopping to chat with Stannock.

Odd, Paige thought. *Major Stannock is his brother and the King's son. Why would I not acknowledge the heir to the throne, and tell him of a message from his father to his general, which will no doubt affect the wars and himself in the northwest either good or bad, unless the old king is really addled as some say he is.*

"I'll do as I'm told," he muttered to the dragon, "though it's mighty odd."

They sailed up from the mountain at second dawn, spiraled up through the ragged cloud to the brilliant first sun, the most important star and the one with a name – Daemon – and then out over the valley, gyred north and up, until they were lost to sight. Almere and Tevron watched them leave. Her smooth left bicep touched Tevron's shoulder.

She shivered and he put out an arm. "Scared?" he asked.

"Not I," she denied. "Never."

She lied.

Though she burned to discover the contents of the sealed letter, Almere promised to say nothing of the mission to Queen Ericaania or the King. King Hakor, she knew, was unpredictable, and she'd been warned not to excite him with Court issues she knew nothing of, which may only cause a heart disturbance in the fragile man or, worse, a fatal stroke of his compromised brain.

"You're privy to more of the King's secrets than I," Almere said. "Though I'm his favored son's wife, he treats me like a piece of that precious porcelain Ericaania collects from across the Agave Sea. I've never been able to convince him that I'm the equal of any man."

"You're disappointed you aren't a son and heir?"

"I am his heir's wife, a future queen" she insisted. "But in the matter of trust, he puts his faith in you and Stannock as Court advisors. I'm not even part of the King's Council."

"Nor am I," Tevron reminded. "And Stannock, as Major General of the King's men, is often at war and unavailable."

"That leaves no one to properly advise the course of Gracklen's future."

Her brother-in-law cracked his knuckles. "Unfortunately again, the King grows weaker every season. Soon he must relinquish the Crown."

"Not to you," Almere insisted. "Stannock is heir apparent, and he will have the controlling vote."

"King Hakor has no other children or heirs," Tevron said. "Sad that is."

"Sad? I'm fully confident of my husband's powers." She marveled at the easy way of their conversation. Had Tevron had a change of heart? His eyes burned into hers.

"And strength?"

She pushed herself up to her full sixty-five units and planted her feet squarely in front of

Tevron's boots. "Stannock is a soldier who loves war. At home, with Fire-Smasher, I am strong, but my Red is not the strongest dragon, and my mother-in-law will not relinquish her dragon Lockjaw to any other's control. So, I don't feel capable of going to the battlefields to help my husband. He says I would be in the way, and pleads with me to stay home. His mother takes his side yet often goes to the killing fields her-self."

"True. The Queen, like her son, is wild and headstrong and was more so as a girl, I'm told."

Almere cracked her knuckles. "Yet she married the King and is meek with the old man's angry fits."

"She had no choice, girl," Tevron insisted with a gruff tone. "After Malcoom died, she had no protector. Her fate was sealed."

"I sometimes wish I were the King's daughter," she admitted.

"No. The stars didn't align with your birth for that, Almere, you are only the King's daughter-in-law. He was a hard man in his youth but he spared me and he gives you privileges only a man should have."

"I love my father-in-law, the King."

"He dotes on you. He loved Queen Ericaania once, too."

Almere frowned. "He must have, to have pursued her as he did."

Tevron continued, "It's not illegal to have two husbands on Draxxt. Ericaania had my father Malcoom and the King as joint spouses, but Hakor grew jealous. The Picts, I've heard, have many mates. If it were me in the same circumstance as the King found himself with my father, I would share you with my brother."

"Never!" She pushed him away. "I would never have two husbands. And I would never have *you*, Tevron."

"I'm not the dainty man my brother is with the ladies," he said. "How do you see beyond the blood on his hands, though? It puzzles me what you love in a man who kills for a living."

"He's a major general in the King's Army. I'm proud of that, and he's an advisor to the King as well. He will be king one day. *That's* what you're jealous of, not me, his wife, but how to get to power by climbing the ladder; the King has put faith in him."

"The fair Stannock will never be king. You won't allow that, little hellcat. You want to rule and Stannock will be your pimp."

"I am not the heir. But I will rule with my husband," she declared.

"He will be but a – a – gigolo. A sycophant. To the King, and to you."

"Go to Hell," she cursed.

He laughed and walked away. "As Stannock's wife," he taunted, "you will have weak children. If any at all."

The remaining dragons began to leave the castle, fanned out with their throbbing colored wings to darken the sky as they pulsed on air currents above the valleys beyond the King's mountain.

"Beautiful," Almere remarked. She never tired of the sight. The Lords who rode those mounts looked for trouble in the valleys and hills of Gracklen, looked for Picts or Trolls or signs of a scattered army returning home, any news of the northern wars along the border and the seaside. Tevron possessed no dragon now, nor did he wish to ride. He felt content as a king's advisor and to plot and plan at Court, his greatest attribute.

"I'm afraid our enemies push always closer to the castle and the walls of the mountain." Tevron frowned, his dark face furrowed in thought. "The Picts have exhausted the riches of the sea where they've lived since time began. Our land must look promising and rich to them. They've pushed their strong crafts off the islands and made desolate the coast."

Almere agreed. "Now it's time for them to pluck the ripe fruit that is Gracklen."

"We've always had trouble with the Picts and the Trolls." Tevron swirled the flask of ale in his brown hands and drank.

Almere frowned. "They lived here before our people made their way from their ships into the badlands of Draxxt. They had enough in their Old Lands across the sea, but they were too lazy to work it. Instead, they chose war."

"True," he agreed, nodding slightly. "We should have killed them while we had the chance."

More blood, she thought.

"They were always more powerful, but because they had no common law they were divided. Each tribe to itself." Tevron revealed what he knew of Pict history. "That saved us an attack from a united front."

"Like they have now?" She sidled away from him, his presence like a magnet, strong and overpowering, almost hypnotic. How she hated him!

"Yes," he confirmed. "They're united under the great Troll, Mindbender. The Picts follow him, and so do the rebel Trolls, the giants of legend."

"Why aren't you at the wars in the northwest, brother?" she asked, scuffing her boot along the rocks at the base of the Great Hall. "Are you a coward?"

"Yes," he confessed simply and sat down. "I'm a thinker, Almere. I know what I want. I have a plan, and it doesn't involve war."

"What then? We just agreed the enemy is united against us."

"War is for bloody fools," he spat. "I'm not a fool like my brother or his father, the King. Our mother, too, is a fool, soaring the evening skies on her beast only to rid herself of the King's company."

"What *are* you then?" Although this man frightened her, she was genuinely curious. "What would *you* do?"

"I would offer them land," he said. "That's what they want. The useless land along the coast and along the northern isles. They'd be satisfied with that if we moved our people out. Our people are outlanders, along the northwestern strip, we could move them back into the valleys where we could keep an eye on them, tax them, control them, and the Trolls and Picts could have the coast and the rough terrain northwest of that. The Picts like to hunt and fish, and the Trolls depend on the Picts. I know they'd be satisfied with that."

Her forehead wrinkled. "For how long?"

"That's the point. Until we grow strong again."

"Until King Hakor passes on? Until the sick old man dies?" Almere smacked her fist on the top of a nearby wall and dislodged pebbles, which bounced down the cliff and off the side of the mountain.

Tevron smiled. "It would buy us time."

"It would buy us only more trouble later, and they'd grow strong, and hungry, and lean, with eyes that would measure our wealth more covetously because they'd be closer. No, Tevron, you're wrong."

"I'm not wrong. Your husband is a fool and so is the King."

"What have you done?" She cocked her head to one side and pursed her mouth. "Where's Paige now with the message? I saw him saddle the red dragon early this morning. They flew off to the northwest. What are you up to now, with your sealed message from the King – what's in it?"

Tevron wiped his mouth with a grimy hand. His thick lips curled upward. He drank again.

"Something's wrong," Almere decided. She sprang to the top of the wall and whistled. A nearby dragon, not the absent Fire-Smasher, spiraled down from the eye of a sun. She threw a saddle onto his back, mounted him, and was gone before Tevron could stop her. He stared, his mouth open, as she and Moonraker melted into a gyring dot in the distance.

She was gone, to the northwest, to seek Stannock.

While there on the valley floor, hundreds of mega-units from the battle, lay the small red dragon, struggling and down, and Paige motionless on the rocks beneath, his saddlebags beside him. In one, the message that would seal the fate of the kingdom.

Chapter Four

"Moonraker," Almere called, "Down, boy! *Fly down!*"

The red dragon, lying broken on the floor of the canyon, craned his neck to stare with blurry eyes at the descending beast and rider. He thought about tragedy and great literature as his tail brushed the still body of his rider.

"My words fly up; my thoughts remain below." Half knowing what the words meant but sick to the huge heart of himself at the blood that streamed across the rocks here in the valley, and the import of the tragedy, the little dragon croaked what once he'd heard from his father, what he now repeated. "My thoughts remain below."

He had failed. His mission was to fly with the boy across the many valleys of the King's country and find the battle. He'd known what he must do, but he'd gone down in mid-flight, the boy and saddle too heavy for the fierce down-drafts from the sandy hills – the currents of air from the warmer valleys whirled them both around and bashed their soft forms against the rocks below.

He had failed, and his rider lay motionless beside him in the canyon.

Since he'd hatched from his mother's egg, he had never felt so helpless. Something was wrong with a rear leg, twisted and bent under his belly. His head swirled in and out of consciousness. He flapped his wings and felt the currents lift him somewhat. The other dragon and the girl were descending, swirling on the treacherous air currents that swelled up from the canyon.

A thin membrane slid over Fire-Smasher's orbs. He lost consciousness.

Fire-Smasher, the young red dragon, lay curled in a miserable heap beneath the sand-stone cliffs of Marlbrex. His eyes were closed and the flame in his throat but a whisper of smoke. Where he lay, the translucent scales of which his mother was so proud, shimmered grey and dull in the afternoon dust. His rider, the boy Paige, sprawled brokenly beside the little dragon about six yards distant. A snake basked on a nearby rock, warming in the sun, and its tongue flickered as it tasted the fetid air, hoping for small rodents nearby, no risk to Fire-Smasher nor his host. Fire-Smasher's sensitive ears picked up the beating of Paige's heart and he smiled to himself – the boy was alive.

Shouting from a whirlwind of air high above, gyring ever closer to the rocks and cliffs where Fire-Smasher and Paige had gone down, sank a dragon of mightier proportions than the red dragon, great talons and mighty thighs extended to land. Fire-Smasher could not groan nor could he move. His senses alerted him that his beloved princess was near. He struggled to open his eyes, to bleat at least a final note of prophecy, for he feared for her life in a wartorn land, but his fall had proven too much for his slight form, and membranes closed over the twin jewels of his eyes. The snake slithered closer, testing the air.

Almere leaped from the saddle and ran first to her beloved dragon, ice churning in her gut as she leaned over the still form. Sour bile burned her mouth as she gazed at her former mount. They had vaulted together the hallways of air, turning as one in the night to order the guards to open the gates of the palace as four moons rose in the southeast, signaling an end to another day of comradeship. A little love snuffed out here, she thought, and touched the dragon's fractured shape. Her mortal ears didn't pick up the rhythmic thud of Fire-Smasher's heart under his leathery coat. She whirled. Her iridescent cloak brushed his outstretched body. She unclasped the brooch at her throat that held the cloak and arranged her garment lovingly over her dragon's tender neck and chest. All she could do for him now, Almere thought and her eyes misted. He lay so still, his head at a curious angle, tucked into his shoulder which had been so strong and vital in happier days. Ever ready to do her bidding when the reins brushed him and her clear voice called, together in the bird-blue sky all day, vibrant between her thighs through the shouting air.

Now his bed was the grit and rock of the Marlbrex cliffs to the west, while his rider groaned and scrabbled in the dirt not six yards away. Paige's right hand clasped his saddlebags as though they held the jewels of the legendary Armgado Mines.

Almere bent over Paige, checking for a breath or a pulse. She swabbed his blood-covered face with a piece of her sleeve. She was relieved to find the blood oozed from a superficial wound on his head. His left arm twisted at an odd angle beneath him. The three suns glowed together through a crevice. A light breeze flickered through Paige's blond hair. Grass stirred amongst the rocks. Almere prayed.

Paige opened his eyes. Later, Almere was to remember two things: Paige had broken a bone. And the small red dragon lay very still in the dust of the canyon, far from home.

"I don't need help," Paige muttered and broke away from her probing hands as though the bones in his body were of no accord. "I have to get to the battlefields where Prince Stannock labors. I have a message for his general, from the King himself." He pulled himself to a seated position. Scratches streaked his face and dirt smeared across his cheeks and forehead. Blood seeped from a cut on his scalp. His left arm hung uselessly at his side. Groaning as the damaged limb twisted beneath the thin fabric of his shirt, he used his right hand to position it, and a bone poked through the broken and bleeding skin. With effort, the boy fastened his saddlebags around his slim waist and tried to smile. He failed, and his glance fell on Fire-Smasher's inert form.

"Your dragon's dead," he muttered, voice shaking in time with his trembling body. "Wasn't strong enough to take the updrafts from the cliffs and the dust storms from the south. I should have taken a stronger mount."

Almere set her jaw. "Lean on me," she whispered. "We'll return for my pet after we've settled you in a medic's tent on the battleground where you were headed."

His damaged head tilted and broken, Fire-Smasher heard the calm beat of Moonraker's wings as they accelerated up into the cooling air toward the north, where Almere's husband Stannock fought and perhaps would die. Fire-Smasher might die, too, here in the unforgiving orange sand, where he was left once more alone.

The thin membranes shut again and mucous formed on the small dragon's eyes. He mumbled epic poetry in his torpor, but his breath caught in smoke in his throat, and he couldn't groan. His mistress had taken the boy first. Her cloak cooled his neck as the second sun's rays beat down on him, prior to evening. He knew the comfort of her cloak would keep his body warm, too, through the long cool night. After that, what then, of his mistress and their love? He was immobilized and left for dead.

Seldom do dragons know fear. That night, Fire-Smasher felt afraid, and deep heart-wrenching despair and loneliness were his companions in the grit and rocks of Marlbrex Cliffs. In the cool of the evening, the snake swarmed to his nest in the undergrowth. All was quiet.

With the boy slouched in the saddle behind her, Almere flew on Moonraker from the
canyon. Paige's rucksack was all they had room
for other than themselves. In his hand, the servant clasped the gold sealed letter from his king,
blood-spattered but intact.

They flew northwest, to the wars and
Almere's husband, and his commanding officer who would open the message and change
the course of the war. Would change their joy
to anguish.

"My master Tevron has access to the King's
private chambers. He's a very special advisor to
the Court." Paige slid his good arm across the
other and grasped the letter with both hands. "I
know what the letter says."

"What?" Almere smacked her heels against
Moonraker's broad sides. His wings beat rhythmically, driving them spit into the wind quick
to the battle and her husband, who *could not*
die. Could not, like the youngest dragon, take
a breath and then not take another.

"Tevron," Paige groaned. It was a statement.
His blank eyes widened at Almere. There had
been a plan. The King incapacitated. Almere

in the Great Hall, taking charge, Stannock her husband dead, and Tevron toppling the King's guards, with the inexperienced Captain Devvid left second command in Stannock's absence.

"What is it?" Her voice carried on the wind that screamed like her thoughts past the plunging wings of the dragon. "Give me that letter," she ordered Paige. "Give it to me right now."

"No," Paige refused. "I mustn't stop. I will take it to the general right away and the general will read the instructions from the King and..."

"And what? What!? You little shithead, useless turd, he'll do *what*?"

"You may have saved my life," the boy acknowledged. "I know that."

"I couldn't save my dragon first. I'm sorry I found you both, maybe he survived somehow, maybe you would have died, Paige, if I'd chosen differently. I wish you would have died. I think I know what Tevron's done and I want that letter."

He shoved the letter into a pocket of his pants.

"I'll find it," she promised.

He groaned and tightened his grip on the saddle. "I'm stronger than you."

"You're not. You're hurt and you're weak, and I'm a strong woman, watch me now."

They careened over the top of another mountain and the Agave Sea loomed ahead. Fires lit the beaches. Four white moons circled the Draxxt heavens. The battle sputtered on ahead of them, illuminated by moonlight and the last of the suns casting a glow in the south. From the beaches, a few mega-units to the eastward, Picts and giant Trolls advanced. Empty now and burning, wooden craft bobbed in oily waters. Almere leaned across the shanks of her dragon to see individual soldiers, the front of the line, where the foot soldiers struggled, the tents of the officers, the pits where they kept their dragons, useless now without trained men to ride them. Stannock would be with his men; she was sure of it.

She saw the general's tent, white with the flag of Gracklen limp on a tattered pole. Moonraker circled the tent.

"Give me that letter," she ordered. Paige leaped from the dragon's back. He sprawled on the grey-white sand. An officer appeared from inside the tent. He seemed to be of some importance since he wore a general's badge. Gasping a few muddled words, the servant scrabbled on the sand and with one hand clenched in a bloody fist, proffered a stained envelope.

The general's tunic was also blood-spattered. He'd just come back from the front lines. He'd ordered his men to fall back; the front lines were too dangerous – all dead or routed. They were losing the war.

"This wax is sealed with the impression of the King's ring," the general noted.

"Read it," the boy gasped and laid his head on the sand. The general motioned for his healers to tend to the messenger and disappeared back into his tent. Weary soldiers were straggling back from the front lines. A moment later, face grim, the seal broken, the general stared at Almere and the dragon. Almere had leaped from Moonraker's saddle with such force that her ankles twisted. She didn't notice the pain.

"Where is my major?" the general asked a soldier, who limped past and leaned on his longbow.

"At the front lines, sir," the soldier replied.

"Quite right," the general whispered. "He is a good man and a valiant soldier."

"Will we all die, sir?" Paige moaned as they took him away on a stretcher to a waiting med-carrier dragon.

The general didn't answer at first.

"Some will," he replied. "It is time."

Chapter Five

Almere couldn't leave her dragon apparently lifeless in the sand at the Marlbrex cliffs. The battle over, she plotted how to remove the precious form. Moonraker was the obvious choice to transport such a cargo back to his home in the Imperial Palace where he could be given proper care or perhaps (dared she think it?), a proper burial. The Queen seemed particularly interested. Not knowing the story of her deceitful son who had forged the King's seal, she lamented over Almere's tale of her downed dragon and its courageous journey to the northwest on the day of their final battle.

"Take me with you, Almere," urged the Queen. "I know some herbs and where to find some fine strong pieces of wood for a splint. We can't be sure Fire-Smasher is really dead. I know far more of such matters than you about the remarkable healing powers of a dragon."

"He didn't move, and I couldn't hear a heart-beat," Almere insisted. "I'm sure he's dead."

After the excitement of battle and the shock of Tevron's deception, she felt entirely numb. She could feel no emotion nor even gratitude for the Queen's offer, nor sorrow for her lovely companion. Nothing. Something wet traced its path down her frozen face, and she wiped away the tear with a trembling hand. That surely didn't come from her dry eyes, eyes which had seen horrors and more only yesterday, on the rocks of the Marlbrex cliffs, and later on the beaches of the Agave Sea. The medics had treated her sprains and burns with soothing ointments and salves and elastic bandages for her ankles. Stannock, her darling husband, and Tevron's servant Paige, were still in the infirmary with so many other wounded and dying soldiers, too many to be counted.

Her faithful mount, so young, this little bit of love, had been snuffed out, she thought. A tear trickled down her cheek. She pondered the old legend of the Dracaena, a human / dragon hybrid female who would be born in the Age of Peace and save their planet. Was it a myth perpetuated by old witch women on frightened children? She had often thought that Fire-Smasher, wise beyond his dragon age, knew more of the legend than he let on. Often they had caroused together through shouting halls of air, oblivious to the bearing of sons and daughters to the kings who would send them off to war. The legend was a great solace to their people, who watched every royal birth for a portent such as the marvelous Dracaena, half lizard, half human. Almere had left her only true companion and confidante to lie broken in the sands of Marlbrex. She feared for their future, the small speaker of epic poetry and Minth dreams, and the future Queen of Gracklen.

Queen Ericaania returned with a rucksack stuffed with herbs, bottles of spring water, splints and bandages. As well as gold coins and something that looked a lot like Tevron's swastika, made of gold, and a little bag of gold dust. "We'll take Lockjaw," the Queen announced. "He's the strongest mount here in Gracklen."

Their journey was measured by the march of the three suns across a blue bird sky. Finally, dusty and hot, they spied the distant cliffs and began their descent.

"No, see, I was right!" Almere shouted insistently. "He's so still and lifeless, Mother. My cape still covers him. He hasn't moved since yesterday morning. This is the snuffing out of a little bit of love from my life, the only solace I had."

"Believe only half of what you see and nothing of what you hear." Ericaania sprang from the saddle and leaned over the unmoving form, its soft grey scales glittering as the second sun set.

"My words fly up. My thoughts remain below."

What?? Almere clutched her throat. "I've heard that before. He said that before. He's alive! But what does it mean, Mother?"

"It's an ancient text from an ancient author, Shakespeare, brought with us millennia ago when our ancestors came to Draxxt and settled here. '*Words* without *thoughts* never to heaven go.' He's saying that he doesn't repent and therefore, Almere, his words are meaningless without thought behind them, and he won't go to heaven. His sins won't be forgiven."

"My Fire-Smasher believes in Heaven and sin? His father, Lockjaw, must have taught him that, from the old memories long ago when such things were part of our beliefs. But he doesn't repent? What would such an innocent creature have to repent of – what sins? He's surely innocent."

A membrane slid open over Fire-Smasher's sapphire eyes. He trembled, stirred, and sighed. Almere flung the cloak from his neck. "He's alive! Please, Mother," she begged. "If you can heal him, do it now."

The Queen bent over the injured dragon, who tried to stand with a broken leg. His eyes slipped closed again.

"He's losing consciousness," Almere said. "He must have been saying his prayers, lying here, thinking that he can't be far from death. Faery-dust taught him a belief in a Heaven where good dragons go after death. The verses must have meant something to him at that time."

"I don't know," the Queen uttered. "He's very hurt." She stirred a bowl of tepid broth and put it to his mouth. He gagged and spit it out. He did the same with the flask of spring water she offered. Both women used some of the water to wash the blood, sand, and grit from Fire-Smasher's body and wings.

"His wings are not torn," the Queen observed. "That's good." She rummaged in her rucksack and brought out some foul-smelling herbs, which she tied in a bundle and applied to his wounds. "These are *charaka sushruta*," she explained. "The herbs also strengthen when given as a tea."

A meager fire burned at her feet, sparked by a blast of warmth from Lockjaw's nostrils. The tea boiled, and Fire-Smasher was able to choke down some of the unfragrant potion. The Queen splinted his broken leg. Fire-Smasher moaned. "Good boy," Almere murmured. "Good boy."

The Queen drew a makeshift tent over the dragon's body to shield him from the third sun's rays. He swallowed some spring water from a flask this time and gulped down some of the broth. Almere sprinkled gold dust on his scotched throat and dangled gold charms from his shimmering neck. Ericaania placed a pile of gold coins in a pouch suspended from Fire-Smasher's armored back, near the area where scales began to glow red, purple, blue, and green, and the grey shimmer gave way to a glorious tail which swung across an expanse of sand.

Lockjaw breathed fire and smoke into Fire-Smasher's mouth and the red dragon responded with small puffs of smoke and flame.

"It's remarkable!" Almere exclaimed. "Mother, where did you learn these healing arts? You are truly a magician."

The Queen smoothed her greying hair from her high forehead. "I'm a healer," she admitted. "Don't tell Hakor. He wouldn't approve."

"Those long trips you take daily?" Almere asked. "Where do you go, Mother? It's not to cuckold the King, I know."

"No." Ericaania's face appeared drawn and her mouth slid to a thin downward curve. "I love the King. But his kingdom is poor, and the people are desperate and in want because of the long wars to the northwest, which affect us so much even here this far eastward."

"So you've studied to help them in their misery?"

"I try," the older woman said. "That's all one can do. A few herbs, a few potions, some charms. The dragons, too. I care for all the creatures I can on Draxxt, and I'm not alone."

"A secret society?"

"Shhhh, child," the Queen admonished. "I caution you not to speak further of this matter. After all, it's against the law to use herbs and potions and charms unless one is a medic."

"Or a witch."

"That's against the law, too." The older woman pushed a lock of grey hair behind her ear and bent over Almere's mount. "Punishable by death."

"Did Fire-Smasher know? Lockjaw must know. He's my dragon's father, and Faerydust must know, too, as Lockjaw's mate. Not only epic poetry was shared, I think, Mother. The charms and gold came from far away, from the Armgado mines, and dragons had to transport them, perhaps in the dead of night."

"'My words fly up. My thoughts remain be-low.' It makes sense, now. He was on another mission, and he didn't know what the letter con-tained but must have thought it was another secret service he was doing as Lockjaw often does. No wonder Fire-Smasher volunteered so readily to transport Paige for Tevron. He must have thought it was another royal prerogative."

"Yes, possibly." Her mother-in-law spooned more broth into the red dragon's mouth. His wings began to beat. He struggled to stand. "Easy now, little one," she cooed.

His breathing, once labored, became smoother, rhythmic. Lockjaw reached out a massive clawed hand and stroked his son's side. Fire-Smasher's blue jeweled eyes flashed and sparkled. The moons were rising and the night grew cooler.

"Take off the blankets," her dragon whispered. "I want to go home."

"Dragons have remarkable healing powers, and this one is young and strong." Queen Ericaania folded the tent, poured more ointment into his wounds, and placed the medical supplies into her rucksack, which she fastened to Lockjaw's saddle. They stayed with Fire-Smasher until nightfall and then the healer and Almere strapped him to Lockjaw's strong broad back. As they rode, Almere petted Fire-Smasher behind his scarlet gleaming shoulders, whispered a verse in his ear, and they soared through the air to the lights of the outer walls.

"You're not a bad dragon. You have not sinned," she assured. "You did good." He seemed to smile in his torpor, and a wisp of smoke trailed from his nostrils. "The old ways talk of sin. It's simply an error. We miss the mark." He smiled again and puffed flames gently from an open mouth. "It was the Prince's error, not yours, and we will learn of it later. You're obedient and young, and your rider was inexperienced. Don't blame yourself, Little Red."

He puffed and clung to Lockjaw's back. "I'm happy," he praised. "You came back for me. I knew you would, mistress."

Chapter Six

The general, who was a good man, said to the Captain by the tent, "Tell Major General Stannock, Prince of Gracklen, to stay at the front line and do not retreat."

"What, sir?"

"Tell him," the general wiped his forehead. "Tell him the King requests he fight to the death, he and all his men, and do not retreat from the peril that is ahead, nor fall back to safety behind."

"That is the King's orders, sir?"

"Don't question it," the general said. "We are warriors."

"That means death to the major and his men, sir."

"Heaven knows that, Captain Devvid." Stannock's commanding officer spun on his heel and strode back to his tent.

Almere listened, blanched, and cursed her husband's brother, who, she knew, had forged the King's signature and forged the King's gold seal. In his ambition, he had murdered his brother and the best of the King's Army.

The giant Trolls poured into the camp, plundering as they came, and the blue painted Picts shot burning arrows into the midst of the scattered Gracklen army. There were five thousand of them, and a few hundred noble men and women to hold them off.

Almere whistled and the dragons wheeled. She leaned and whispered into Moonraker's ear. He snorted fire, bucked, but obeyed, and whistled to the rest what they must do to win the war and rescue the Prince. The riderless dragons swooped onto hundreds of cooking pots for the King's Army, full of hot oil, and hoisted them with crooked talons to the sky.

A risky move but it might work.

The enemy murdered as they advanced. *Where was Stannock?* Almere tracked the messenger the general had sent to the front with the false message until she could no longer follow him, then she saw her husband. Her stomach churned. She felt a warmth in her groin at his dear, familiar shape, and then she forgot any sensation at all other than cold, hard anger. Next came the fear.

He was at the front of the line, not falling back, hacking with two swords at a line of Trolls. Hundreds of Picts shot burning arrows into the thickest part of his army. His men fell like stars on an August night. He was bloody and bleeding and held one leg at an awkward angle. His boots were slashed and his tunic hung from his shoulders in shreds. But he fought. Oh, yes, he *fought,* and Almere warmed with pride and overwhelming love, joy, at seeing him again after four cycles of the moons, and how brave he was. He was here, he was alive, and she would make sure he stayed that way.

At that moment the dragons of Gracklen rose into the air and dropped their cauldrons of boiling oil and greasy water on the hordes of Trolls and Picts.

Almere looked behind her once.

The Queen screamed from the back of her dragon, diving again and again with the rest of the Lords of the Castle, striking with burning arrows at the hordes below. Ericaania had followed them from the castle, brought aid to their cause with her men and their mighty mounts! Crimson fire erupted from every dragon's throat; the enemy streamed back to the beachheads and onto the waiting boats.

On the sea, their corpses bobbed and burned. On the beach, intermittent globs of burning oil spilled onto the exhausted foe from circling dragons. Ericaania screamed again, like a Valkyrie, and shook her fist at the last of the setting moons as a new sun rose from behind the southern horizon.

"It's not over!" Almere shouted, but the Queen and her lords were gone, flaming dots in the dusty dawn under double moons, another set of suns rising in the south and east, all quiet below except for the groans of injured men and the enemy. The dragons were unscathed.

Moonraker swooped to what had been the front of the line, where many of their king's Gracklen warriors, too close to enemy lines, had been burned by boiling oil and died. A lone figure slumped over a spear stuck in the sand. Ice churned in Almere's belly. Was he impaled on the spear? He wasn't moving. Then she realized he was leaning on the weapon for support, and he was alive.

But who was it? Could it be –

Stannock looked up. He saw his wife sliding from the saddle of her dragon, slippery with blood, dirt, and mud. She limped to him. He thought she had never looked so beautiful. They embraced. The battle was over.

Chapter Seven

The feasting continued for fourteen days and thirteen nights. First, the whole roast boar brought into the hall on a huge wooden platter, with ripe fruit in its mouth and surrounded by young beast baked in its mother's milk and platters of exotic fruits, everything in and out of season imported from across the Agave Sea on swift boats. There were slabs of guinea hens and wild turkey, huge mounds of scented rice, sweet potatoes, asparagus, tomatoes, carrots, green beans, and cabbage; all kinds of pickled and fermented foods; fresh baked breads of all descriptions, some unleavened and some as light and high as an angel on a cloud. There was butter and garlic and spices and herbs, chocolate and puddings and cakes and pies.

Under awnings and umbrellas in case of rain, great tables were set outside. All the land of Gracklen received invitations and they all came to feast at the King and Queen's expense. The war was over.

The King's people ate well.

They were surprised on the fourteenth day, at the twelfth hour, when the grand bell rang at the entrance to the castle, such entrance being at the base of the cliff, not where the dragons and their riders habitually flew.

"Their Majesties have no time to be distracted during this period of celebration," the stewards said to the lone figure who stood there, dressed in tight black pants and a silver coat. "The favored son has returned from the wars victorious, and his injuries have almost healed. The enemy has been driven back past the shores of the Agave Sea. Gracklen is at peace."

"I've come to apologize," Tevron explained. His demeanor was repentant. "I've been living with the Picts and don't like it."

"Try living with the Trolls," his brother sneered, peering over the steward's shoulder. "Or on the other side of the planet, in the outback, where you can eat prickly pear and drink from muddy waters."

"Please," Tevron begged, his face looking tired and humble. "I'm sorry."

"Do you know the gravity of what you did, Penis Face?" Almere shoved her husband aside, blue eyes flashing beneath a mop of wavy black hair.

Stannock threw one arm around his wife's shoulders and with the other hand held a glass of red wine. "I love that gown," he said to her. "Or is it the hat? Something's different."

"It's the shoes," she answered. "Good solid ankle boots with straps."

"Oh? Very sensible."

"My ankles don't hurt today and thus I smile more."

"Very sensible," Stannock repeated. "The sprains and burns will heal shortly, with the healers' ointments and your sturdy good health." He shooed away the stewards, who stood with swords drawn against his brother.

"What about *me*?" Tevron wailed. "The Picts have a price on my head."

"I know the King wants you here, bro," Stannock said. "I'm not sure he cares if you're alive when he gets his hands on you."

"What did you do to the Picts?" Almere smirked. "Just curious. I thought you were on their side."

"No, of course not, never was," Tevron denied. "I just thought I was doing the best thing for the kingdom. I'm a patriot, Almere. I'm sorry, Stannock. I never meant to get you killed."

"Oh?" Stannock sipped at his wine. "That's a surprise. Brother."

"I don't think you're wanted here," Almere scoffed . "I think the King has a price on your head. Better take your chances with the Picts."

Tevron leaned against the gatepost, thumbs hooked into his pants pockets. His black curly chest hairs gleamed in the low light from the open top of his tunic.

"Where's your crooked cross, the swastika?" Almere asked. "The one you wear around your hairy chest. For protection. You need protection now, bro."

"I traded it for beans last night. It was valuable, forged with silver and gems from the Armgado mines, and taken from a Pict by my father before his death. I left it with a trader, who'll return it for a price."

Stannock beckoned. The stewards with their pikes and swords edged closer. "Seems to me that was a good trade. No excuse for a dead man to have a talisman as fey as that. I've heard it belongs to the Fairies, just the same, and only the Queen of the Fairies is free from the curse."

"I think there *is* a curse. Talk to the King and Queen," Tevron whined. "I'm begging you, Stann. Nobody in the land will take me in and nobody will feed me. My love life stinks. I'm losing weight."

"Looks good on you," Stannock commented.

Almere grinned. "Tell you what. Come with me to the women's quarters and we'll hide you there until the King calms down. Mariette can look after you. We'll see to it that food is set aside for you after every meal, not what you're used to, maybe, but it's edible. Not what the pigs get."

"That's *excellent*."

"Here, wear this." She threw a billowing cape around his still broad shoulders and pulled the hood over his eyes. The cape was blue, like a flower. Like Almere's eyes, he thought. No time for that now. That's what got him into trouble in the first place, lust for power close to the King, women and – Almere's eyes and Almere's face and Almere's breasts and how she moved. He swallowed and followed his brother and sister-in-law to the upper floors of the castle, careful to avoid the banquet hall.

Mariette looked after him in the women's quarters, changed the sheets on his bed and washed his clothes, brought his meals. Made sure he had something to read. Made sure he had something to do. Hid him well when the Queen's other maidservants poked their noses into her room.

It *was* her room. Not surprising, then, that after a few nights he also shared the older woman's bed, which creaked under the considerable weight of both of them. She was worried the Queen would hear, her room being directly below Mariette's.

"You have eyes the color of a cat's," Tevron said one day. "Your hair looks like the straw in the King's fields."

"That's not a compliment, dearie." Mariette was folding nightshirts. She whipped one out of the ironed pile, folded it with a snap, and placed it in a drawer. "You've got to do better than that to keep a good woman."

Tevron leered. "What about *this*?" He grasped one of her ample boobs in his hand and played circles around the nipple. "Now the other one."

She pulled away. "Any fool's servant can do better than that."

"Stannock's unavailable." He laughed.

"You know," she said and slapped another nightshirt into the drawer, "if you piss me off, handsome, you're out of luck at the castle here. This was your last resort and you know it. I know it. We all know it. So crawl back under that rock you slithered out from three weeks ago and clean yourself up."

He sobered. "Sorry. Sorry, Mariette. I didn't mean anything by it. You're right. You're hiding me real well; it's more than I deserve. More than I expected."

"And sharing my apartment, too? You bet."

"I got a favor to ask," he said.

"What is it?" She frowned.

"Next time Almere takes a bath, I want to know."

"Why?"

He winked. "You know. That peephole in the corner."

"You son of a bee. How'd you know about that?"

Tevron crossed his arms. His shirt pulled tight across his chest. "Let's just say I've been here long enough. I notice things."

"You poke around when I'm not here, bet your gauntlets."

"Maybe. Well, how about it?"

"No." The ironing basket was almost empty. Her cheeks bloomed pink.

"No?"

"It ain't right. That's all and that's it in a walnut shell; you got no right to be prying around our next king's lady. You're lucky you got a bed at all, let alone a bath to yourself when night-time comes. Or meals. Don't go pushing your luck, lover man."

"Lover man," he snickered. "That's good."

"Besides, there isn't no peephole in the corner."

"Okay, if you say so, luv."

"Now take this basket to the laundry room," she ordered. "You'll fill it up soon enough. Never saw a man wears so many clothes on his back as you. Tuckers me out just finding them for you. Good thing the guards aren't too observant about what they put in their wash from one week to the next."

"Yeah, they're good husky fellows; most of their shirts fit me well. The pants are a bit tight."

"Well, you're a well-proportioned fellow, I got to say that," Mariette mused, her cheeks pink again.

"I'm going to miss you," he said. "I'm leaving next week."

She raised hay-colored eyebrows. "And where would you be going, smart britches?"

"My brother came to see me today. All's forgiven. Blood is thicker than water and the King's forgotten pretty well what I did. Stannock thinks he'll take me back. I'll chance it. Can't live like this forever. Not that it hasn't been great. Wonderful, actually. Appreciate it." He kissed her chubby cheek and pinched her buttocks.

Mariette slapped his hand. "Go away with yourself, now. Well, I'm glad to hear that. Can't stay here with me, hiding you away, trying to use my peephole." She paused and stammered. "That is – my – trying to say things like you did."

"I know," Tevron said. "Thanks. And you know…"

"What?"

"It's time I got my own dragon back. Mine was lost in the wars. All the women got dragons, the Lords—"

"I know just the one. Heard about it the other day, it came up from the Valley, a brand new dragon, already tried out, maybe a bit careless about its burden – you'll have to wait 'til it grows some, though. Went down a few moons ago, with its rider."

"Did it kill anybody?"

"Matter of fact," she continued with a hand on her hip, "almost died itself, it did. Heard tell it crushed a servant."

"Yeah." Tevron nodded, recognizing the story. "I heard that, too. But I heard the dragon was dead."

"All's well that ends well," she said. "You'd know that better'n me." Her pale eyes glinted. He cupped a large boob in one hand and sneered.

"Interesting." Tevron pondered the situation with pursed lips. "If he's alive, he might be too stunted to be of any use to me or my lady. The little dragon may not live." He raised his black eyebrows and wiggled them. "Dragons can talk, can't they?" He pinched his lip. "Also, dragons grow real fast, and this one is special to my lady. Maybe a matter of politics to soar on the back of a mount beloved by the future queen?"

Mariette snickered, her portly body jiggling. "*Your* lady? Last I heard, she was married to the king-apparent."

"My brother, the hero." Tevron glowered, thumb circling her nipple beneath the coarse fabric of the yellow flowered apron. His erection strained against his body-hugging, silky court pants, and Mariette licked her lips, looking at the thick pole she had enjoyed so recently.

One more time for good luck, she thought and wished her mistress well with this one. He would be king before his brother yet, she thought, and it would be well if the little princess knew that and counted her eggs carefully before she placed them all in one basket. Mariette would help her, as a good servant should, and this interlude with the brother would be good for the maidservant, too, if she played her pinochle right. Another boisterous tussle on the soft, fragrant straw mattresses, and Tevron packed his bags in preparation to leave the women's quarters.

"Good luck with the mistress," Mariette called after him. "Her dragon might not be so easy to ride, the mount that almost killed a manservant. But you ride well, Tevron." She snickered. "I'd look up Red, if I was you; he ain't such a little dragon anymore. He knows secrets nobody else knows, and a good 'un taught him to speak. He's grown, too, good and muscled now, I hear, and still growing."

Tevron's stay in the servant's quarters hadn't gone unnoticed. He and Mariette made a lot of noise at times, the guards' clothing had been missed, and he ate more than his share of the palace food – as usual, though, his luck held, and he rejoined his brother and the court the next day.

Chapter Eight

Stannock was right. The King forgot about Tevron's insubordination. In his mental lapses, the King had almost forgotten there'd been a war. Tevron slipped right back into Court society, except for Stannock and Almere who held a grudge, he thought, even though they told him they understood his ambition as neglected older brother and forgave him.

"You only tried to kill me," Stannock pointed out with a dismissive shrug. "No big deal, right?"

"Stann. That's not fair."

"No. No, it isn't."

"See, I told you," Tevron said. "It's not fair. I love you, little bro."

"Yes, Tevvie. We love you, too."

We? Tevron lifted his eyebrows. *Hot damn!!!!*

"So what are we going to do? We're both advisors. The King never comes out of his room and he won't take visitors anymore," Tevron noted. "It's like we're the King."

"We have to respect his position," Stannock replied. "We have to accept his authority as long as he's still around. No matter our personal feelings. Until the Council decides he isn't king anymore, he's still our sovereign."

Tevron squared his shoulders and sucked in his gut. Almere had just come into the room. "You're on the Council. I'm not," he reminded his brother.

"I'm only one voice. And honestly, I don't want to be the one to get rid of the King. He's been monarch for more than sixty years now. It would kill him if he knew."

"Hmmmm." Tevron pulled at his lower lip and scratched his head. Something to think about. Stannock continued, "He trusts us. I don't want to abuse that trust."

"He trusts *you*," Tevron pointed out.

"What's happening?" Almere asked, limping into the room.

"We're trying to kill the King," Stannock said. Tevron laughed.

"That's not funny, Tevron." His younger brother sucked on his teeth.

"I might have something to ask you." Almere faced the stocky dark man. "Like did anyone talk to the King about what happened at the battle, about stealing his seal?" She glanced at her husband, who threw gold coins into the air then jingled them into his pocket. "And what did he say?"

Tevron measured her with his eyes. She was strong and taller than he, but he easily could take her. He chewed on his lower lip. "I think if Hakor wanted to tell you what he thinks, he would."

"No," Almere said. "I'm not sure he would. I'm just a woman in his eyes, after all. Not worthy of his confidence."

Tevron plucked a yellow blossom from the planter and lobbed it at Almere with the blue eyes and the wavy black hair, the woman he adored yet hated. Stannock grunted and lunged toward his older brother.

"I would not say anything to anyone if I were king and had been so stupid," Tevron said.

"I would not tell *you*, either, little black-haired witch." He whistled all the way home to dinner.

Mariette watched from her peephole in a corner. She wasn't happy. *So sorry for myself. The hunk loves the King's daughter-in-law.* There must be something she could do. Jealousy flickered in her base mind, and she plotted her revenge.

Chapter Nine

Although beloved by the King, and loving in return, Almere knew the monarch was even more crippled emotionally than physically. He was far older than his wife, Queen Ericaania, and with the knowledge of his failing powers came fierce jealousy and suspicion that approached paranoia. They shared a royal bedchamber, each with a vaulted four poster bed, thick carpets on the floors, and tapestries adorning the circular walls. The doors were extra wide and supported by great carven posts on either side, to allow the admittance of the King's wheelchair. A woolen blanket habitually covered his knees to ward off the chill of the dank walls and drafty porticos. He wore the velvet coats and trappings of his office, his arms and shoulders huge against a barrel chest, his fingers thick and strong as he propelled his wheelchair about the confines of his room.

"You're an impressive sight, my dear," Ericaania said. "The Pict who took Tevron's swastika cross must have trembled in his boots to think his king demanded it back."

"Nothing stands in the way of my personal guards," the King said with pride. "I don't need to go out of my chambers to put the fear of Gracklen in them. Tevron was very foolish to give away what turns out to be an amulet of such powers."

The Queen nodded and put another stitch in the tapestry she was decorating. "He didn't know it was magical and he was desperate for food."

"He could have used it to be a master thief."

"A charm which renders its bearer invisible has always been a legend in our time."

"It was on its way to the master Troll, Mindbender, when my guards intercepted it. Can you imagine what Mindbender would have done with it? He would have started the war all over again, stealing and looting. The charm has a radius of several hundred yards and it renders our dragons invisible, too. Invaluable." He snorted and shifted his large bulk in the wheelchair. "All these years your son wore this powerful swastika cross and didn't know what he had around his hairy neck. Impossible. The man's a fool."

"Tevron is as Tevron does." The Queen's voice was soft but her eyes betrayed hurt to hear the insults against her son. "He has a fine mind but it's clouded by pride and greed, I'm afraid. My dear, you're right about one thing. Mindbender would have used the amulet for his own dreadful purposes. Will you return it to Tevron now?"

The King blew a rude noise through his nose. "Of course not. You're not getting your hands on it, either, you cheating whore."

"What? I have never cheated on you, Hakor," she said. She took another stitch. A storm settled about the King's crippled brain. She had started something she ought to finish but knew from experience it was useless to argue with her husband.

"Except with Tevron's father?" *Liar.*

"Malcoom was my lawful husband, and I married him before I ever met you, Hakor. You know that. You destroyed him."

Malcoom died poorly. He was a fool. Or was that his son? No, the son still lives. "The love of your life." He snorted again. "I should have hacked the head off his son, too. Now look what it's come to. They're all plotting treason against me, and Tevron most of all."

"That's not true," the Queen said. "Your sons and daughter-in-law are very loyal."

"Maybe." He glowered at his wife. "But you're not."

"That's not true, Hakor. Please don't accuse me of these things which I have never dreamed of doing to you. I love you. Always have, even through the worst days of our union when Malcoom was ripped from my arms, and I lived in terror that our son would suffer the same fate."

The King wheeled his chair closer to the woman he had married thirty years ago. "You know we had an agreement."

"I kept my side of it, and so did you. Until this crazy talk today, I thought my sons were safe in their home."

"It's unnatural," he rumbled. "The son of my own loins I don't suspect, but this dark and brooding lad, he's up to no good. If I could remember more often that his father was a traitor and a cuckold, cuckolded by me and who knows how many others? Like me now, cuckolded by the son I took in under my wing, through the goodness that flows through my veins, because you begged me to spare Malcoom's boy."

"Cuckolded!" he shouted and bashed his fist onto the table so that the porcelain knickknacks flew to the floor and shattered.

"What are you talking about, Hakor?" The Queen's face went ashen. She was standing opposite her husband, on the other side of the marbled black mirror. "I've never been unfaithful. What do you mean about my son? That's absurd and disgusting. I don't know where you get these ideas. They're crazy." It was the wrong thing to say.

Spittle flew from the King's mouth. He backed her into a corner, roaring and pounding his fists on the walls so that the tapestries ripped and some hung crookedly. "I'm crazy, am I?" he shouted. "I'll show you who's crazy! You think

I don't notice that you leave at the same time every morning, riding that big dragon of yours into the day, and don't come back until well after nightfall, and then tired and wild looking? You think I swallow that story about neighbors? And that son of yours sulking in his rooms at the other end of the courtyard, stirring up trouble with Almere and our hero son who fought in a battle at the end of the world? When he's too lazy and cowardly to even ride a mount in a northwesterly direction for fear that he'll be forced to fight?"

"He's an excellent advisor and is needed here."

"He's an *excellent* advisor," the King mocked, raising his voice to a roar. "Is he *excellent* in bed, too, you who meet him every day in the valley for *sex*? Which, need I remind you, *I* don't get from you, and haven't for fifteen years." He wiped the spittle from the sides of his mouth. "Fornicator! Adulteress! Incestuous witch!"

She gasped and stepped aside. "I can't believe you. I can't believe this. It is too absurd. Please stop."

"Please *stop*," he repeated. "*Please* stop. Why don't you look at yourself? Maybe it's your dragon who's getting a little in on the side."

He stopped finally, panting and gasping, his head and beard lowered to his chest like a bull getting ready to charge. His hands reversed their grip on the chair and he rolled backward to the doorway, blocking any hope of exit.

"Hakor," she pleaded with him, hazel eyes brimming with tears. "I have always loved you. I loved you when Malcoom was alive and I love you now. Please don't do this to yourself."

He shook his head as though to awaken himself. "You may be right," he mumbled. "I'm sorry."

"It's not the first time," she reminded him. "Really, I'm tired, dear."

"Go to bed then." He raised his voice again and called for his manservant, Jon, to put him to bed. He had exhausted himself. In an inside pocket of his velvet tunic lay Tevron's swastika. He palmed it in one beefy hand and swung it around his neck on the thick silver chain. There was a secret to its powers of invisibility, which the Pict had revealed only when his nails had been torn from his fingertips and his wife's soles had been burned to blackened stumps. The Picts were a stubborn race. The King admired them greatly and remembered his stepson's plan to evacuate them and the Trolls to the land in the far north, relocating the Gracklen settlers. *An excellent plan,* he thought. Good thing he'd thought of it. Just like that dark warlock, his stepson, to claim the idea for his own and try to make himself ambassador to the lands of Mindbender the Troll.

Not a bad idea, though, and Mindbender was an honorable prince. He had been a worthy adversary on the field. That useless son of his own loins, Stannock, had done nothing right until he married the girl, Almere. Maybe Stannock was getting it on with his mother, too. Hakor wouldn't be surprised. His ablutions done for the night, with Jon's expert help and guiding hands, he settled his huge bulk into the equally huge bed and closed his eyes. The incantation he had learned from the Pict scrolled across his closed eyelids, on a red and black background. He would reveal it only to Stannock's captain because this captain had made sure that his cowardly son remained at his post when he was about to flee the battleground.

Yes. I can trust Captain Devvid. I'll send him on a mission tomorrow, to follow my wife, and to report back to me at the end of the day. He'll have to be invisible, and I'll make sure he has the fastest dragon. I think my wife's dragon Lockjaw will do, but the queen will be suspicious if I force her to switch dragons. Maybe Fire-Smasher, if he's healed. The King opened his eyes. His wife sat on the edge of her bed on the other side of the room.

"I'll need a dragon tomorrow," he said. "I can use Fire-Smasher or Moonraker, or one of those beasts that have come back from the wars."

"Okay," she said. She briefly wondered at his purpose but he was a mercurial man and she feared angering him with questions. "Okay." She rolled into bed in her ankle-length white night-gown with the ruffles at the throat and wrists. Her loose grey hair fell in waves around her shoulders. He thought she looked rather beautiful, but was too exhausted from his tirade to tell her so, and a little ashamed.

Tomorrow he would know her secrets. Already the events of the evening blurred in his mind. She had provoked him into an irritable and quite understandable outburst for a few moments, that's all. He was tired and weary from entertaining, and from the responsibilities of his office and the war, of course, so recent but even so, beginning to recede in his mind. He wished he had spoken to that girl tonight, that sweet young girl, what was her name? His son's wife or paramour or whatever, the girl who always made him feel good about himself. He couldn't quite remember her name, nor the name of his sons, but it would come to him in the morning.

His wife, he knew, had purposely provoked his anger; it was fitting that she remain on the other side of the room, silent and weeping in her bed that he so generously provided for her. He clung to bits of incantation that floated about his head – there was something important about the silver and gem-encrusted dragon's charm, and he didn't remember until he unclasped his fist and felt the amulet. Oh, yes. The icon of invisibility. His wife's son was a warlock and fool and would lead to the destruction of his mother. Neither could be trusted. His son's name? Tevron. Not Stannock. Tevron.

He rolled over in bed, straw mattress rustling and bending under his weight. Jon placed a glass of water on the nightstand and turned a table-top lamp to its lowest setting. He folded the King's clothes and laid them on shelves, padded on soft feet to the door, and gently closed it on his way out. A vast darkness settled over the King, punctuated through his eyelids by the light his servant had left burning. He chuckled in his sleep.

Chapter Ten

Captain Devvid's sinewy form melted onto the muscular back of Moonraker, a few minutes after the Queen had gyred to the sky on her Lockjaw, off to the west. He thumbed the secret amulet of silver and jewels, muttered the incantation the King had taught him, and both he and the dragon disappeared. The world appeared as though through a pane of shimmering glass in his invisibility, but he could hear perfectly well.

When beneath his thighs Moonraker ascended and turned westward, following his mistress through instinct and guidance, Devvid smiled at the simplicity and ease of the chase. He could see his Queen on Lockjaw far ahead, a dot almost lost in the puffy white clouds above Gracklen. They banked to the right and then to the left, soared over badlands and rugged snow-capped mountains, then to the south and then back to the east. He kept on, never losing her, the pace steady. The three suns of Draxxt burned through the white cloud cover. He looked back once and saw a bird following, its wings beating and petite in the distance. The planet beneath him wavered through the sheen of invisibility. Then, suddenly, eastward again, closer to the King's palace.

He pulled up on the fiery reins, puzzled at the chase – or perhaps it was a game? Perhaps the Queen spotted him and played with him for sport? No, Moonraker existed as a pane of glass and his own limbs were shimmering and translucent.

The queen's mount banked sharply, down to the valley, down to a rough-hewn building surrounded by shrubs, trees, familiar animals, and a gaggle of farm buildings. Down. She alighted at one end of the huge house, which swung open on great hinges. Devvid and Moonraker glided to a clearing in the forest near the house. He left his invisible mount in the clearing with instructions to stay until he returned.

Moonraker attempted to follow his queen into the buildings where fifteen or twenty people swarmed around her. "No," Devvid commanded, thumbing the dragon charm, and Moonraker, obedient, responded to his art by lying down in a sunny spot in the clearing. Devvid found he could see his dragon well enough, as though through a shimmering lake, but he had been assured that no one else could break the dragon's code of the charm or see them. He crept, just the same, to the edge of the clearing and then hid in some shrubs near an open window of the great house. His Queen's mount hunched tethered outside and the Queen conversed with a group of women inside a great hall. He moved closer to the open window to make out what they were saying. Certainly, the King's suspicions proved inaccurate. The Queen was engaged in some sort of secret rendezvous, but it wasn't with the Picts or with any man.

Devvid peered through the open window and, shocked, couldn't believe what he saw. On the vast tiled flooring of the house sprawled a massive green troll. He knew from the size that it must be Mindbender, the Troll who had gathered the Picts and Trolls together for the first time in their history to fight as one. Surely the Queen was a traitor. Then Devvid saw the women gathered around the Troll and the many jars of ointments in their hands and the herbs of all descriptions simmering in bulky iron pots on a central stove. Scruffy small animals and even wolves purred and rubbed on the women's bare ankles, wandering in and out through the open doors, and on the window ledges, black birds bobbed their sharp heads. The Queen stood in the midst of this, gloved white hand stroking a large spotted feline.

The Troll appeared immobile, did not seem dangerous at all, and golden blood seeped from various wounds on its body. Bandages dressed its bulbous head, and one of the women applied a potion to the cuts on its hairy green scalp. The captain counted the men and women who milled around the Troll and outside amongst the buildings. There were groups of thirteen. Certainly, this was a secret society of witches and warlocks, or healers, probably, rather than anything sinister. They worked on the Troll, splinting his limbs, rubbing ointment into wounds, bandaging and sprinkling sparkling dust on his head, chanting as they did so. In another area of the great hall, tail protruding from the open-hinged wall, sprawled a red dragon. Scales shimmered beneath the sunlight streaming through the roughly hewn open windows. Its right front leg was splinted, healing scars crisscrossed its head and body, and it *purred.* The dragon's muscular chest and thighs strained against its tight armor.

The captain pressed closer to the gaping hole that served as a window. The Queen seemed to be in a position of leadership. He watched as she stroked the Troll's face with a cloth soaked in oil. As the day wore on to evening, the captain ran from one opening to the next without detection, for the dragon charm seemed to muffle his footsteps as well as render his body invisible. He took copious notes. He sketched what he saw in a coil notebook, invisible as well beneath his invisible rucksack. He recorded in notes and sketches almost all that he heard and saw.

It seemed that Fire-Smasher had gone down in Marlbrex and was left for dead by his rider. The healers located and recovered him and the

Queen and Almere transported him here. He was almost healed, stronger and more muscular than before, as dragons grow quickly and heal even faster.

A group approached the tableau from one of the outbuildings. The captain gaped. Almere was amongst them, and she grasped the muscular red dragon's talons in her hands, stroked its translucent wings, and sprang to its back without the benefit of a saddle or ropes. Devvid thought she had done this before. The red dragon, no longer the smallest dragon, crawled outside the hinged wall of the building, sprang to its feet in the surrounding shrubs, and raised rainbow wings.

The Queen and her coven applied salves and ointments to Mindbender's wounds. The Troll sat up, smiling, revealing sharp golden teeth like a ferret.

"I'm so grateful," he said in deeply accented Gracklenese.

"Only three more sun cycles and you'll be well enough to return home," one of the healers informed him, smiling.

Fire-Smasher, weak but stronger, strode on firm steps around the house, Almere on his back, and snorted epic poetry from a dry throat.

"Prophesy!" the coven called, and Devvid, leaning closer, heard from the dragon of a future alliance between Trolls, Picts, and people, a division of land in the barren areas toward the northwest, a permanent home for the Trolls and Picts at last, the human settlers relocated in a lusher and greener valley near the Armgado Mines where there was plenty of work, and an alliance with the King's Palace.

"That is doubtful," said several, and others dismissed the proposal. "It will never happen. It's impossible to find a peaceful solution to this war that has gone on for decades, and only now is won by the Palace. King Hakor will never make these concessions to his sworn enemies, even for the purpose of lasting peace."

"Tevron," intoned Fire-Smasher. "It's Tevron's plan."

"Then the King will never accept it," they argued.

Almere called from Fire-Smasher's back, "I was there when he said it. It's a good plan. It can work."

"Long live King Stannock!" called a few of the braver hearts.

Ericaania scoffed, reminding them of the battle recently fought and won at so dear a cost.

The captain pressed his face against the rough wood of the window opening, willing himself to be quiet. He felt as though he would burst with excitement. What a plan! No more wars in the northwest, no more scuffles with the Picts nor the Trolls. All united under Mindbender and the Gracklen King.

"Sounds ideal," the Queen agreed, raising the giant Troll to a sitting position. "But the logistics are probably impossible. Our people would have to agree. Your people would have to agree. A few dissenting voices could start a riot. And the King – well, he would never agree."

"I have an idea," Almere said, from atop her mount. Fire-Smasher snorted rainbows and smoke. "But I'll have to talk to my husband and his brother."

"Wait." The Queen held up one white-gloved hand. The others grew quiet and waited for her to speak again. "As you know, in five days the first of our three suns will shine through a particular slit in the Great Hall here, in this vast house our ancestors built, and illuminate a spot on the opposite wall, beginning the Day of Ascension for all who celebrate the Old Ways. It's the one day of the year when we all gather together under one roof, all those from the valleys beyond and the mountains beyond those. We'll have a general meeting of all leaders and a vote from the covens. That way a democratic process will decide which delegates will approach the Palace and how we'll go about it."

A general cacophony of sound erupted, all speaking at once. Devvid could not make out who said what until the Queen raised another white-gloved hand and they grew silent.

"My husband will never agree," she stated. "But I have two strong sons and Almere. We'll meet before the Day of Ascension together, the four of us, and perhaps it's time my husband the King, regrettably, steps down. I'm sad to say it, but I have reason to believe he has reached the limits of his rule."

"He won't do it voluntarily," several of the witches called. "And he'll put us to death if he knows. Our Old Religion is illegal in Gracklen. It's too much of a risk. We won't let you take that risk alone, either, Queen Ericaania."

"I'm willing," she said simply.

Almere, listening, turned Fire-Smasher around with reins of fire and smacked her heels against his sides. "That's my king and father you speak of," she reminded them, her voice breaking. "I won't let you do that to him." All the people were silent. Not a sound disturbed the clearing.

"There, behind the east wall, by the window, in the *calendula offisinalus*! Do you see what I see?" she called.

The captain blanched behind his shimmering plate of invisibility. He thrust his notes and sketches into his tunic and stepped back, noiselessly, he thought, but Fire-Smasher and Almere were on him in a bound.

He could tell they couldn't see him, though; they were acting on instinct and perhaps a charm of their own that sensed his presence. He brushed past the questing dragon and his rider and ran on soundless steps to the clearing in the forest where his mount shimmered and shone. Quickly, Captain Devvid sprang to the saddle, thumbed his dragon talisman, and they bounded soundlessly and invisibly vertically above the clearing, gyred east, and home.

King Hakor awaited word in his chambers. Devvid was rewarded with a royal smile, so uncommon and so charming, but knew in his heart he'd done the wrong thing by returning to the King. Surely as he'd predicted, the King heard the prophecy of alliance and suspected the healers of heresy and treason.

"Burn their houses," he ordered. "Arrest the healers, including my wife."

"I have my orders, sire," Devvid acknowledged. "My battalion will carry them out. But sire—" He hesitated. "Wouldn't it be best to wait five days until they're all together for Ascension Day? Burn the buildings around them, arrest those who escape, try your wife the Queen for treason, but be patient, sire. We can get more fish in the pond by waiting."

"Very good, Captain Devvid," the King said. "A good plan. I am a patient man." He rocked his wheelchair back and forth. "And my wife – I'll look after my wife." The King smiled again, but without mirth. Devvid shuddered. What had he done?

Chapter Eleven

"My dear." The King held out his massive arms to his wife as she ventured through the inner chambers. Captain Devvid had departed moments before. Rich tapestries adorned the walls and colossal twinkling chandeliers dripped their colored candle wax from soaring ceilings. Sprinkled across the expanse of the floor were polished pieces of jeweled tile. Creamy billowing couches lined the walls, accented with velvet and silken pillows. His chair purred on thick golden wheels to the center of the room where he presented the Queen with a smile bereft of guile. Startled and suspicious, she held out her arms to her husband in return. He took her in a bear hug and whirled her about in a crippled dance in his chair. "I've been so remiss," King Hakor growled. "I've missed you, Peaches."

"Why, what have I done?" the Queen said, pleased. "How have we come to this kind of welcome, Hakor?"

He tickled her neck with his beard. "Love," he said. "Remember, darling? Love is peaceful and kind, love never fails. I've failed you these past many moons and I've failed our sons. Trust me, dear. Our poor marriage is now a matter of history – trust, love, and fidelity always win. I've been unkind. Come to your puppykins." He clasped her close in his arms. She returned his embrace and kissed him passionately on the lips.

"Oh, Hakor." She breathed into his neck, arms tight around his barrel chest. The blanket slipped off his lap as she cuddled close. "I've been so lonely. Remember how it used to be with us? Our sons saw it, when they were young, loving parents and a loving husband. What's happened to us?"

"I'll make it up." He murmured into her ear like a rosebud beneath the soft swirls of grey. She cuddled close, closer. "Close your eyes," he whispered.

Hakor slid a dagger from a scabbard at the side of his chair. She trembled with desire, eyes shut. The dagger hovered poised at her back. *No!* he thought. *Poison! No one will know or suspect. She is well liked in the kingdom. I will blame the healers.* He slipped the cruel blade back into its shaft and pushed his queen away.

"Go to your bed," he teased. "I'll be in shortly."

"But, Hakor – you're so mercurial. I'm puzzled."

He patted her butt and purred into her ear. "Like it used to be. Wear something pretty. Maybe that silken crimson corset?"

"Oh, yes."

"The black dangling pearls, the scent of lilac and musk? Light the candles, angel. We'll share a drink together. First." He chuckled and patted her butt again. She giggled and flung her legs from his lap. She stood and stretched.

"First a bath," she sighed. "A long hot soak in lavender bubbles and musk. I'm cold and dirty from my long ride tonight."

"Ah, yes." He rang a tiny silver bell at his side. Jon, his manservant, appeared almost instantly at the door, swinging the huge beams inward, and strode toward his king. Ericaania glided through the curtains at the other end of the hall, throwing a kiss to her monarch as she went out.

"Sire?" Jon took the arms of the wheelchair and prepared to escort the King to his nightly ablutions.

"Jon," said the King. "I can trust you."

"Yes, sire."

"Anything?"

"Anything, sire." Jon's thin face twisted in a smile. "I've served you since you were a boy, my Liege."

"Yes, you are very faithful, Jon. I need a favor." Jon waited silently. "There are many herbs in the kitchen to help me sleep?"

"Yes, sire. You need something now?"

"Something a little stronger. Something that can't be detected by our medics nor by taste. Do you understand, Jon?"

"I understand, sire. No problem. I'll fetch it immediately. In a cup of wine, sire? And may I say, you look particularly fine tonight."

"Our lady needs help tonight." The King whirled his chair about and selected a crystal goblet from a corner case. "A small capsule will be best."

"I understand, sire."

Later, the King slipped the poison into the goblet and placed it into the locked armoire by his four-poster bed. Tomorrow would be soon enough. Tonight, he would pleasure himself and his Queen. He would deal with Jon in the near future. The old manservant would not live to tell of the King's deception. Old men's hearts were notoriously fickle. Especially when pierced with a dagger dipped in yellow bitter tincture of cu-darene.

King Hakor smiled. It would be a good night.

Chapter Twelve

Mindbender, the King of the Trolls, stood in the thatched humble building of the healers. His green gnarled head brushed the ceiling beams, though they were twelve deca-units high. Many moons had passed since the Queen of Gracklen found him on the battlefield and brought him here, far from the marauding dragons of her liege and the covetous Picts who might forage for treasure amongst the wounded and dying.

He ventured into the moonlight and held a huge hand in farewell to the healers who surrounded him and wished him well. They pressed gold and healing herbs and ointments into his rucksack as he prepared to leave. Then his many-leagued boots strode from the clearing in two extended steps; he melted into the fragrant cool night illuminated by two moons which shone all the way to his land in the north-west called Many Waters. The journey was long, but Mindbender felt stronger than he had since he was felled on the battlefield by a blow from a dragon's mighty jaws. He silently thanked the good Queen Ericaania, cursed her husband the King, and made his way northward to the Arm-gado Mines and then to his own home. He was joined on his march by the Picts who had supplied Tevron with sanctuary after the infamous battle won by his brother's clan and the Queen's dragons. Smaller than he, and brightly painted, the Picts entertained Mindbender with stories of the Palace gleaned from the Queen's talkative son.

He learned of Tevron's plan to unite the lands near the Agave Sea with the Gracklen kingdom and thought to himself, *It has merit.*

"My liege," chattered a blue Pict at his elbow, "are you sure you're well enough for this trip? It's many, many mega-units of walking, and you've recently escaped almost certain death. If it weren't for the healers, you'd be dead and our lands would be leaderless."

"Supply me with rations and arms," Mindbender ordered, "and we'll rise again unless the Prince's plan can be put into action by the mercurial old king. I think he can't be trusted. But it's land we want, and if they can supply us the badlands, we'd be happy with that."

"For the moment." The Pict simpered and hoisted his sword from its scabbard. "We'll fight to the death once again. When we're united again and under you, my liege, nothing can stop us."

"Oh, yes. They stopped us, all right," the Troll said. "Peace is a tenuous thing; the Palace knows that. The old crippled king is a fool but not that much of a fool. They'll march on us again to keep us from their lands, but if we have land, why, that's all we want."

"True enough," the Pict said. "Prince Tevron is a peacekeeper, I believe, not like his warring brother."

"Half-brother," the huge Troll corrected him.

"Yes. Well, we fight for land and respect."

"That, too," the Troll said. "Respect." He flexed his newly energized limbs. "I don't know why the Queen would have saved me."

"She knows it was politically wise," the Pict surmised. "She knows if you had died, the land of the Picts and Trolls would have been dangerous and unpredictable. We are a warring lot, and we're proud of it. We need your protection, and we need our lands still."

"Yes, she knows a political solution is vital. Now the fog rolls in from the sea."

"We near the ends of the land," the Pict said. "Your magic boots have transported us many leagues of distance tonight. The fourth moon is setting and the first sun, Daemon, is rising in the south. "Our charmed Pict legs are a match for your magic boots. But it's time to rest."

"Rest I won't until I reach my home and hearth." The Troll continued to stride without seeming to tire. "Did you return the talisman to the Prince?"

"Yes, the Prince traded it for food." The Pict simpered. "Not knowing of its power. I returned it to his manservant, Jon, the old man's name was, who showed up in the inner courts to collect it after I'd sent word."

"Why did you give it back, knowing it renders invisibility?"

"We don't need it, and the Prince did. He isn't our enemy. Our enemy is his brother and his brother's troops, and the old unpredictable king."

"Besides," the Pict continued, "as you know, it has a curse. Better the curse be on the kingdom than on us."

The Troll laughed. "I know about that. Yes, the magic always comes with a curse as well as a blessing. As most things do. We must accept that, but I have my cloak and my boots and don't need the dragon talisman, either. It'll be interesting to see how the curse works out in the kingdom."

"I think it even now is making its way toward the old king and Prince Tevron, too, who won't know how to control it. If Tevron has it, he won't let it go, but I suspect the old manservant of treachery. It's sort of a joke with us Picts. Treachery to treachery." He laughed.

"The curse has to do with love, right?" The Troll faltered as they approached a bog, the first sun's rays shining in the murk and mud. He took a tentative step and stopped.

"What's wrong?" the Pict asked. His comrades also stopped at the edge of the mire, which would not have deterred Mindbender in his better days.

"I'm tired," Mindbender said.

"Told you." The Picts collapsed on a muddy slope and passed around flasks of stale water.

"Love is a two-edged pike," the Troll continued. "I don't have anything to do with it myself. I live alone, my wife lives leagues away and natters at me even so from a distance. I get no peace when she is around."

"The King may feel the same way," the Pict said. "And the talisman sure has that curse, anyone who's ever used it has felt the two-edged pike of love pierce his heart and destroy his life."

"Good or not?" The Troll sank onto the slippery bank. He laid his head on his arms and sighed.

"Ha, ha," the Picts laughed together. "You think your wife lives a distance away and still nags and torments you? Wait until the Prince feels the power of the amulet. He'll give it away again, and not for food this time either, but to be left alone."

"I hear there's a maid." Another Pict carried gossip from the King's court. "Someone in the castle."

"Ha, ha. He'd be wise to throw away the charm."

"But the King could use it. He already has been cursed in love."

Mindbender sighed. "The Queen is the one cursed, and by her husband who grows older and more vicious every day."

The blue Picts all sighed together. "I remember when these lands were peaceful, and love filled the air."

"That was so many seasons and more ago that it has moved from the memories of most of those citizens in the kingdom. To the detriment of the ruling classes," Mindbender bemoaned. "If King Malcoom were still here, the politics would be a different thing. And the young Queen, how fey and charming she was!"

"Still is," the Pict said, and the bog in front of them bubbled and churned.

"Time to go on." Mindbender rose and plunged into the fetid mud. They reached Many Waters before the third sun set that evening.

Chapter Thirteen

"We'll wait four sun cycles for the Day of Ascension when the healers are all gathered together in their great hall, then we'll arrest them and charge them with magic and poisoning the Queen." King Hakor ran his thumb along the edge of his cup and glowered at Captain Devvid. "The Queen is no better than they."

"Arrested for poisoning the Queen?" Devvid asked. "But the Queen is alive and well."

"Not for long, Devvid," the King replied, the secret perched on the edge of his lips. "Not for long." He chuckled.

"I see," Devvid said, wary of the King's intentions. "So we wait to burn down the healers' house?"

"Yes. We want them all together. Screaming and charred. There are barrels of oil in my storehouses. Prepare the strongest dragons to carry it, dump it on the buildings, and set fire before they can escape. If there are survivors, bring them to my dungeons where they can be tortured and killed."

Devvid remained silent in response. Then he spoke with hesitation. "The charm – It twists in my pouch. I think it's enchanted."

"Of course, it's enchanted. It makes us invisible. We'll use it again."

"I don't think that's a good idea," Devvid said. "I have a bad feeling about it. My wife grew sick last night, for no reason she is failing, and my children are ill. I blame the charm."

"Give it away, then." The King shook his head and shrugged. "Give it back to my stepson. He'll know what to do with it. It's his in the first place. If it's cursed, let him take the curse."

The King cackled and threw back his head. "There's good reason that magic and witchcraft are banned in the kingdom. They're all cursed. All of them. They'll die, and they'll die cursed by their own witchcraft and magic. I'm sorry we had to make use of it, Captain. You ought to give it away as soon as you can. I think it came from the Trolls long ago. They didn't want it. They're wiser than my foolish son."

"He'll take it back. He always wore it around his hairy black neck," Devvid said. He didn't like the older prince. Didn't trust him, and he didn't trust how he looked at Princess Almere when his brother, Prince Stannock, was fighting valiantly in the Troll Wars to the north.

"If he's cursed, it will spare me killing him." The King stroked his grey mustaches as he considered his luck. "He's too much of an oddity in my court. The fool wants to make peace with the Picts and that great hulking Troll that has brought them all together from Many Waters and beyond the Agave Sea."

"They want land," Devvid said.

"Always it's territorial," the King replied, wiping a glob of spittle from the side of his mouth with a gnarled hand. "They're savages. They can't have my land. There are settlers on that land."

"It's a meager living for them." Devvid shrugged, formulating an argument to put forth. "They wouldn't miss it if they moved from the badlands. But we don't want the Trolls and Picts any closer to Gracklen than they are. I agree."

"They've always been a problem," the King complained. "That fool Malcoom was too soft with them. He started it, really, by making concessions and giving them Many Waters in the first place, and the shores on the north of the Agave Sea. Now Malcoom's son is as foolish as his father."

"Court intrigue," Devvid murmured.

"What?"

Devvid quickly silenced himself. He shuddered inside at the turn the conversation had taken. Perhaps the King really was mad? Rumors of fits of violence and rumors of madness were whispered throughout his kingdom. If young Malcoom hadn't died, he might have tempered Hakor's strange cruelty. Malcoom died in bed, his head severed from his body. Reports said there were orders from the Queen's new husband, Hakor. Orders were given, then no more competition for love or wrestling for power in a kingdom where there would have been two monarchs. An inside job, the Trolls, had been blamed, and a savage war ensued.

The captain sighed and rose from his velvet chair.

"It's late. I'll leave you now."

King Hakor held out his jeweled hand and Devvid kissed it. "You'll do it?" the King asked, referring to the burning of the healers, their animals, and their house.

"Yes," Devvid replied, but he meant more – a warning to Mindbender and the healers, and perhaps the Queen herself. He strode from the room, and almost knocked over the King's manservant entering through the polished doorway with a basin in his hand and the King's fresh towels over his arm.

"I'm so sorry," Devvid said.

"No problem, sir," Jon replied. Jon was an old man; he knew where his duty lay, and he knew the consequences. The King had been a cruel boy and now was a cruel man, but Jon had served him and his family for most of sixty planet turns. He would go to his grave with his loyalty to the King intact.

Chapter Fourteen

Stannock surveyed the Big Red Fire-Smasher, as he liked to call his wife's mount, now that the youngest red dragon had gained muscle and virility. In secret, Almere fed her dragon the herbs that her mother had used to revive him at the Marlbrex cliffs. Her old saddle, armor, and the dun blanket were far too small now for the dragon, and she rode him bareback through the rising of the first sun, Daemon, and the mists of the valleys where they swooped and sang, then banked steeply up to the far blue dome of Heaven. Often, she visited the badlands where Stannock was stationed as Major General of the King's First Battalion. They oversaw the settlement of the lands to the north of the Agave Sea and kept peace amongst the Gracklens who lived there as farmers and fishermen. Infrequently, there were raids by fierce painted Picts and their neighbors the Trolls, but in all, the great troll, Mindbender, kept his subjects under control. There was talk of uprising amongst the settlers and their neighbors the Picts, and Stannock's diplomatic and military skills were tried to the fullest as he represented the King and his country to the best of his ability.

"I'm a soldier, not a diplomat," he complained to Almere on the morning of her arrival at the outskirts of Many Waters, where his tent was erected in the midst of his battalion's bivouac. His tent was a soldier's dwelling, not so much different from the general's on the day of the attack which seemed so long ago now, the day the King's Army had successfully defeated the invaders. It was made of white animal skin, furnished sparsely with a single cot and blankets, a table, two chairs, and desk. Stannock's tall form and his sleek blond hair contrasted nicely with his barrel chest, long arms, and bulging biceps. He had his father's beard, though not sprinkled with grey, and his father's temper was lost on him but may be a result not of genetics but of environment, for, as a child, Stannock had been subject to the Queen's gentle hand and her maidservants. His father, King Hakor, had ignored him for the most part until he grew of age to be interesting to the older man: hunting, fishing, and warring. So Stannock's temperament was also gentle, except in battle, which he loved, and for which his father's guards had trained him from the age of ten years.

"I don't kill for the love of it," he reminded his wife. "But war is an art and the arms are a valuable skill. It's what I was trained to do. Not this paperwork, not this diplomacy, not the court intrigue, which I try to avoid as much as I can."

"I was drawn to you not because we were betrothed from necessity at an early age, when my princely father died and my mother ran away, but because we shared in some way a bond of friendship when I first was welcomed into the Palace. Your warring ways never attracted me. I understand, though, that you're a man who was trained to the art and science of battle when a child, and it's all you know as a profession, except, of course, to be a future king." Almere stroked the side of his stubbly face with a tender hand. "I was thinking that we could ride together today, in the sky that is so close to Heaven."

"What's this talk of Heaven, then?" Stannock brushed her hand with his and kissed the delicate fingers. "Are you listening to the Old Religion and its sister faith, that have been illegal for centuries?"

"Of course not." The walls of the tent were thick and provided shelter. The doorway was secured with a wooden plank through which a thick cord of rope was tied. She sank onto the cot, pulling her husband with her. His erection strained against the tight pants he wore as chief officer. She put a hand on the thick pole of his manhood and fumbled with the knots on his trousers. He groaned and fell on top of his wife the Princess Almere, tearing his britches as he lunged, with a knee beside her soft thighs and the other pressing against that secret place which only he truly knew.

"Stannock..." she breathed and began to moan. His fingers lifted her skirt and pulled at the lace and silken undergarment beneath. Almere tore her bodice from her breasts and flung herself against the rough blankets, threw her legs wide apart, and he entered her with a single stroke, his body bounding into the midst of her upturned knees. The cot squeaked but held. Their forms were flung against the leather walls of the tent, in and out, and their cries mingled with the sound of sharp-beaked birds and horny cattle lowing in the fields around the encampment. His guards outside glanced askance at the billowing tent, in and out, and the animal moans that issued from within, the bodies careening in merry lovemaking which the guards themselves had no chance to experience for many sun cycles.

"Heh, heh," an older soldier smirked, and the others responded, "Heh, heh."

Soon there was widespread merriment, and a nearby milkmaid joined in, tickling the chest of the nearest guard through his uniform until he deserted his post and pulled her to him in the shade of a neighboring Thurtle tree. The foot soldiers raised their daily drink rations in salute to their major's lusty entertainment for the day, until the cot inside buckled with a crash and a thud, and the white tent collapsed.

"Damn!"

"Stannock, get off me!"

"Get off me yourself, Almere. I'm suffocating!"

"Hot damn and dragon's breath. The whole damn tent fell down."

"Oh, NO. I can't see, Stannock!"

"I can't breathe!" The sides of the tent bulged and the door buckled on top of the splintering poles.

Fire-Smasher waited outside in a thicket with the other dragons and spread his rainbow wings in celebration of the spectacle. His mistress and her husband emerged from the wreck of the white tent, red-faced and disheveled. Stannock wore his jacket buttoned to the neck and his tunic belted and secured with a sash, though the day was hot. Almere staggered by his side, skirts awry and bodice partially open. She spread her white fingers across her chest to hide the marks of lovemaking. Fire-Smasher snorted and lowered his head to chew on the lush purple shrub to which he was tethered as a symbol of obedience to his mistress. The other dragons snorted, too, and lowered their heads. The soldiers and guards busied themselves with their mundane tasks, and Stannock and his lover began to pull at the remains of the tent.

"Here, now, sire, let us help you." A sergeant at arms beckoned to three or four sturdy fellows and together they brought up the thick tent poles that had survived and the skins to cover them.

"You'll need some privacy, I imagine." The older sergeant saluted then left with his men.

"Yes," Stannock called after them. "Thank you, fellows." His face was red and streaming with sweat. Almere pushed past him and they entered the tent together, glad to be out of sight of the soldiers, who conspicuously turned their eyes away from their major and his lady love.

The milkmaid emerged from the bushes, smoothing her skirts, and the guard staggered out minutes later. Inside the tent, the Prince and his lady tugged at the cot, which sprang erect, and spilled three plump pillows onto the bare floor. They sank onto the pillows, laughing, and Stannock pulled her close to his chest.

Fire-Smasher munched on the shrub, considering what he had just witnessed. A wolf creature howled in the thick of the forest. Fire-

Smasher lifted his serpentine neck and howled, too, then he roared, with great puffs of smoke and fire dribbling from his huge nostrils.

"PISTOL'S COCK IS UP

AND FLASHING FIRE WILL FOLLOW."

Then he broke his silly tether and approached, his head slithering side to side above the dusty ground of the clearing, to the back of the white tent, where he could see, with his great dragon eyes that saw all, the forms of his mistress and her husband inside the tent, engaged again in what had just been a debacle witnessed by all!

The wolf howled. Fire-Smasher snickered, understanding, and dropped his mouth to the ground, where he licked up remnants of spilled beer, and other fine things the soldiers had dropped in their haste and mirth.

Chapter Fifteen

"He can't be allowed to do it." Captain Devvid's voice was soft, afraid of being overheard, for even the walls had ears in the King's Palace. Stannock and Almere, newly returned just that morning from the badlands, leaned closer, fingers intertwined.

"I want your advice," the captain continued. "He is my monarch. I'm a traitor to him now. But I'm faithful to my queen and to you and your princess. I just can't do this, go ahead with a mass murder of the healers in the valley, burn their house around them, destroy their familiar animals, destroy the Queen, I'm sure that's what he has in mind, though he told me to leave her from the killing. I know he's going to kill her, and I heard his mad ramblings. The King is a madman. He'll turn on you and Tevron next, I'm sure of it. We have to stop him."

"You mean force him to abdicate? Or we ought to kill my father?" Stannock's pale face twisted as he thought of possible solutions.

"None of us want to kill the old man. I think the Queen ought to be included in our discussions," Almere said.

"She's in great danger," Devvid agreed. "Yes, she must be told. Let's fetch her right away. Has she returned yet from her daily rides?"

"Yes," Almere said. "She's with her maids in the baths right now, freshening up after her day in the valley. I'll get her. The King's with his counselors in his chambers and won't interrupt us in Stannock's private residences. We have to have time and room to plan, but we might not have that much time if the King is going to act in three days, the Day of Ascension, as the healers call it, when they'll all be together, including our queen."

Looking up at his much taller major, Devvid scooted over and took a seat closer to Stannock. The roughhewn benches on which they sat were adorned with soft animal skins, velvet cushions, and large goblets of wine were set in front of each of the men. Devvid took a draft from his cup and swirled the ruby liquid with a thumb.

"What do you think, Stannock? Could we do this without killing the King?"

"I have an idea," Stannock said. "Almere and I have actually talked about this between ourselves. But it would mean involving the Queen as a healer."

The captain saluted. "Very good. I thought of that myself. Drugs?"

"Yes. But nothing deadly, you understand. We have to talk to my mother. And Tevron, of course, who's now in the settlements in the badlands. I haven't seen him for several days but he's found himself a large cottage and a modest orchard and has traded some of the king's jewels for cattle and pigs. He's become quite a farmer and has quite a legend growing up around himself. Apparently, that swastika cross he wore? It's a dragon's charm, we're told by the Pict who took it in payment for a meal, then returned it to King Hakor."

His captain screwed up his face and rubbed his forehead. "I know that charm," he admitted.

"I have it. It seems to have an effect on those who use it, though, that's not for the good."

Stannock's eyebrows shot up like two blond bushes. "What does it do?"

Devvid considered. "I don't know if I should tell you. The King gave it to me and asked me to use it to follow the Queen on her daily rides, to find out where she goes, and what she does."

"Did you find out?" Stannock asked. "My mother gets away from the King, I would imagine. I can't blame her for that. But what does she do all day?"

"I did find out," the captain admitted, "But I had to use the charm of invisibility to hide away in the valley of the healers, and I saw your mother the Queen amongst them, using herbs and ointments, and ordering them around as though she was the leader of the coven."

"Coven? But that's illegal, has been for millennia, since our ancestors ventured from the Old World to come here on their ships of fire, long since lost and almost forgotten. Surely my mother is courting death if she's involved in witchcraft and healing?"

"She knew that, surely, but they aren't evil, sir," the captain said. "They do good; they heal and treat and cure diseases and set broken limbs. I saw it with my own eyes. In three days, they'll all be together to celebrate what they call the Day of Ascension. I don't know the meaning of it, but it's important to them, and they'll meet in their big house. Probably there'll be forbidden ceremonies, and your mother will be there. That's when the King ordered me to burn the house, with the healers in it, and your mother and those who escape will be thrown into prison and killed."

"Does he expect my mother to be there? Or does he have other plans?"

"No, as I said," the captain began, "Your mother—"

Just then the door banged open and Almere appeared, followed by Ericaania still in her riding clothes.

"What's this?" Ericaania strode across the room with a few long steps and sat beside Stannock. "Why was I brought from my baths before I'd even had a chance to clean myself? What is this, and, Stannock, why are you back from the fields, and what is your captain doing here as well? Almere, what is this?" She snatched a goblet from the table and drank deeply.

"Your habit of drink," began Stannock, "it may be the undoing of you. The King has plans to silence you forever, Mother. We think it may be with poison, to put the blame on the healers, and misdirect the citizens who love you. It would make his burning of the healers' house, and of the healers themselves, plausible to the public. Devvid found a capsule of poison in the King's cabinet next to his bed, he knew where to find the key, and we fear it was meant for you. He searched the King's room as soon as we returned from the field, knowing his mad accusations."

Almere sat next to her mother-in-law, and together the two men and she explained the King's plot to Ericaania.

"The poor man!" Ericaania exclaimed when they'd finished speaking. "He must be completely mad and completely frightened and angry to think of such a thing. I have never hurt him nor been unkind in any way. Or unfaithful. Let me see the capsule."

Stannock proffered a ruby red capsule of clear liquid. The Queen inspected it. "Just as I thought," she said. "It would be undetectable and painless. These poisons aren't easy to come by. I suspect the King has an accomplice."

"Can you replace this capsule with another harmless substance that looks just like it?" Almere asked.

"Yes, certainly, I can," the Queen replied with confidence. She grasped the pill between her thumb and forefinger with white gloves and slipped it into a pouch at her belt. "I have just the thing, or can manufacture it. He'll place it in my goblet tonight, probably, and I'll pretend to be ill and take to my bed. But first, I have a plan how we can force abdication without harming or killing our monarch."

"Poison?" Stannock swirled the ruby wine in his golden goblet, staring at the reflection of candles hanging from the high ceilings sparkling in the bottom of the cup. "I don't see how he could survive that, as fragile as his health is, though he looks to be a huge bullock of a man. His heart is no more than tissue paper."

"I have the thing," the Queen said. "*Manasseh amanita.* It is a rare fungus found only in the badlands, growing on the north side of the Thurtle tree in wet seasons, and doesn't cause death."

"What does it do?" Almere asked. She clasped Stannock's hand.

"It causes forgetfulness," the Queen said.

"For how long, and what kind of forgetfulness?" Stannock asked.

"Memory loss, and the effects have not been noticed to lessen with time." Ericaania rummaged again in her pouch. "I have some here, dried and ready for use. I kept it for Mindbender, in case he wasn't accepting of our offer of truce, while we treated his wounds."

"But he was?" Both Stannock and his captain sat straighter on their benches. Stannock's eyes met the captain's. "I would be willing to negotiate a truce with the Trolls and Picts, even against the King's wishes, if the King were incapacitated and I was on the throne. I think we should call my brother Tevron back from the badlands, so he can be included in a triumvirate on the throne if we can persuade the King to step down."

"I'd like to meet with Tevron again," his captain said. "I have something for him." He proffered the heavy silver and gem encrusted swastika dragon charm, which squirmed in his hand. Almere shuddered.

"I recognize that all too well," she said.

"He wore it for many years without knowing its true purpose nor the curse that I'm sure is on it," Devvid said.

The Queen protested, "I should have protected Malcoom's son and my heir – as a healer myself, and a practitioner of the darker arts, I'm ashamed and astonished I allowed it without seeing its price. I think my son suffered because of it. He is a far better man now that he's rid of this accursed thing. You want to give it back to him? No, I say. Throw it away, into the deepest sea."

"You never told me what it does when it's cursed," Stannock persisted. "You've used it, you say, as an invisibility cloak, but how far does its power extend?"

"Quite far," the captain said. "It covered my dragon in the clearing, and I was unseen until I returned home."

"I know it now," the Queen said. "The curse involves bad luck in love, and not only bad luck, but evil in return for good."

"It's normal and well understood that a powerful dragon charm like this would have a curse on it," Stannock said. "None of us knew Tevron was affected by something evil he wore always around his neck, so close to his heart."

"My poor son," Ericaania bemoaned.

"I know someone who wants it," she continued. "My maid. She has been pining for Tevron since he left her bedchamber."

"An invisibility cloak? Bad luck in love? Would we do that to our brother?" Almere asked.

"Yes." Stannock laughed. "Tevron deserves it. We'll tell him of it in due course. You know how he forged my father's seal to send me to my death? This will be payback for my dear brother."

"No, you can't do that," the Queen said. "He's my son, too. And we now know that he was cursed with a talisman that changed his character so he did this evil thing."

"Cursed, yes," Stannock said. "As well he might be, as well I would have been in death had you and your dragons not come to my rescue,

Mother. Let's give this to his maid Mariette, and see what she makes of it. I think Tevron won't be alone for long." He laughed again.

"I agree only if we tell him within a full cycle of our moons," Ericaania said. "He must choose to rid himself of it, as the rightful owner."

"How'd he come to have it?" Stannock asked. "I've never seen him without it around his hairy neck until he returned home after the feast."

"His father," the Queen answered. "My first husband, Malcoom, wore it and it was plundered in battle from a Troll. Which, we don't know, lost in the clouds of history. It could have been one of the ancient Trolls of old, from whom Mindbender is descended, a giant and a warlock, but we'll never know. In any case, Malcoom soon lay in his chambers, dead, and I pleaded for our son's life, which was granted if the manner of Malcoom's death was never divulged to the public. It leaked out as gossip, of course, but never acknowledged by me nor confirmed. So, I've kept my promise, and Hakor has kept his. Tevron wore the amulet as a boy, as soon as he was old enough to learn the art of swordplay at age twelve, and has worn it ever since. I know he misses it."

"It's as much a part of him as his smoldering eyes." Almere didn't mention her true feelings and thoughts toward her husband's half-brother, not wanting to hurt the Queen nor Stannock. She thought it was an excellent idea to give the amulet to Mariette.

So, it was decided. The Queen prepared a delicious mushroom soup for the King's meal the next evening, two days from Ascension Day, and sprinkled in his bowl the drug of forgetfulness. For her own part, she substituted a harmless capsule for the poison in the King's cabinet. They dined that night like the old lovers they were, and the Queen watched as Hakor slurped at his soup.

"Delicious," he said. "It's been many a year since you've cooked me a meal like this, my dear."

"I know how you like mushrooms," the Queen replied.

"Quite right. Now let's have a toast to your beauty and good health." King Hakor put down his spoon and raised his wine glass. She raised hers. The ruby liquid sparkled in her golden goblet and she drank deeply. Satisfied, the King watched her drink.

"To a long life," he toasted her.

"To many happy memories," she said.

"My dear," The King winked.

"Your soup is getting cold," she reminded him.

"Quite right, my dear." Hakor raised the bowl to his lips and Ericaania watched as the hot broth covered his mustache, dribbled from the sides of his mouth, and slid like butter down his throat. He burped and wiped his mouth with one mutton-like hand. She finished her wine and slumped to the floor.

"Quite right, my dear," the King repeated and rang his little silver bell. Jon appeared almost instantly. "Jon," he said, "clean up this mess, will you, like a good man? Thank you."

Jon took in the scene with pale yellow eyes. "You are right, my liege. It is a mess, and your subjects have misjudged you."

"Yes," the King said, "I'm smarter than they thought. Now, what was it I said? A mess, you say? Quite right. Clean it up, there's a good man."

Queen Ericaania sprawled on the floor and didn't move as Jon heaved her tall body into bed and tucked the mauve lace blanket around her chin.

"Yes. You are a very wise man, and they have misjudged you." The old manservant wrung his hands and bowed as he backed out of the room.

"Oh, Jon. You flatterer." King Hakor coughed. "Now what was it I said?"

Chapter Sixteen

Into the wild, the wild blue dragon sky. Up through the swirling currents of air, until the clouds are below them and the sun above, no haze or dust storms to block their view. Almere clasped with her knees Fire-Smasher's rippling sides while silver and purple scales sloughed off his back and whirled behind like confetti at a Pict wedding. His neck and jaw snaked out below, teeth like massive white swords. His jeweled eyes – at one time burning sapphires – glowed and sparked like huge emeralds set in the depths of ebony sockets. His tail was an armored spear, shot through with crystal, his thrusting thighs sensuous beneath her. His wings beat in an iridescent symphony of color.

Fire-Smasher was magnificent.

Their transport was significant because, in Almere's duffle bags, nestled papers of State to be signed by Hakor's stepson. A triumvirate had been formed in Tevron's absence and with the King's indisposition, consisting of Almere, Stannock, and Ericaania, but awaited Tevron's instructions of his own place in the new order.

The new King Stannock had not yet been crowned. His coronation awaited the will of his advisors, of whom Tevron was chief, having been instrumental in giving birth to the concept of a truce with the Trolls and Picts and a resettling of land for them.

The Gracklen settlers already began to grumble about being dispossessed of their lands in the badlands, and part of Tevron's job while living in the settlement was to encourage farming and fishing in the more fertile regions on the southernmost banks of the Agave Sea and eastward from there. He found that relatively easy to do as he had a natural bent for negotiation, could be hard when the situation called for it, yet was a diplomat when the cause seemed right.

Fire-Smasher carried on his back an unlikely extra passenger and a new saddle wrought from gold, decorated with images of snakes and sparkling with jet and rubies.

Mariette, safe in her cocoon of invisibility, clasped the back of the saddle with arthritic fingers as Almere's dragon dipped toward towering twin mountains, soared between the peaks, and brushed snow-packed cliffs on their way to the open air. A lake green with silt sparkled far below and Fire-Smasher banked on one rainbow wing, plummeted down through the surface, and dove to the bottom like an arrow of fire, Mariette and Almere still clinging to his back. He drank copiously, filtered fish through his sharp, powerful teeth, and swam near the surface to soothe his sunburn. Only his neck, head, and tail showed, starting a local legend of a monster in the lake. Almere and Mariette, invisible and protected by the amulet, screamed with laughter as they sliced through the green, cold liquid that fed into the Troll land of Many Waters.

"How do you like the ride?" screamed Almere as they bucked and soared from the lake to the sky again.

"Miss, I'm doing it for love." The amulet swung between the maid's broad bosoms. She muttered the incantation she was taught at the beginning of the ride, rendering them both transparent but Fire-Smasher, in his magnificence, fully visible. "My loyalty can't be bought," she asserted. "I'm faithful to the old King Hakor, but I'm only a simple servant. I swore an oath to King Hakor when I entered his service from my humble home in the valley, as a girl. Now there's a new king and I have to change my ways. It might be a good thing; it might be a bad thing, I'm thinking, that there's a new monarch there, the brother of my lover, but the old king was his stepfather, and more powerful and kind, I think. At least, he was always kind to me. I had a warm room, a job, fatty meat, bread and hunks of farmer's cheese and sausages to eat my fill. It was a good life. Now? Who knows?"

"Who knows, indeed?" Almere shouted over the rushing wind by her ears, which blew her tousled black curls from her tanned forehead. Her blue eyes sparkled as she pulled on the fiery reins. "Whoa, boy," she said. "We're here."

The maid behind her mumbled a phrase, flicked at the amulet around her throat, and the cloak of invisibility lifted so they could be seen by wondering settlers who, a moment ago, had gaped at a lone dragon settling its bulk near the shores of the Agave Sea. Among them was Tevron, walking his wolfdogs.

"Mariette!" He choked when he realized she wore the dragon's charm – his swastika – which he'd given away for beans. She crawled from the dragon's back and swayed, glaring at him.

"So here you are," she said. "You don't have to come back with us if you don't want to. We have everything you might need here, in Almere's rucksack, and around my neck."

"The truce is uneasy," Tevron said. "I need the authority of the King to validate my case and give me, as his representative, some assurance."

"Don't we talk pretty." Mariette fluffed her grey hair with one gnarled hand. "If you want your dragon's charm, come and get it, lover boy."

Fire-Smasher wandered off to breath fire on a rather large mammal, which he toasted for lunch. Still mounted, Almere slipped off her dragon's saddle, a gift from Stannock, and patted his muscular side. The great spear of his sparkling tail waggled in the sunlight. Under that red, purple, and green tail swung great testicles and a pole of a penis peeked from a wrinkled grey foreskin, like a young elephant creature. Almere's hand slipped to the secret spot and cradled the balls in her hand. They bulged and pulsated, and the dragon's penis slowly emerged from its shaft. She glanced around, but there was no one else in the clearing. The smoky smell of roasted meat tantalized her nostrils.

"Hey, Almere, what are you doing? Come see this." Tevron, with Mariette, inspected the papers from Almere's rucksack and poised a thick stylus above the bottom parchment. "I think I should sign it. It gives me status as the King's full brother, uncle to any heirs, and heir apparent if there are no heirs. I like that. Sounds fair and just to me."

"You'll find that my husband is a fair and just king," Almere said, emerging from the clearing. She wiped a bead of moisture from her forehead. Mariette chewed on a blade of grass and leaned on Tevron. Almere noticed the swastika was not back on her brother-in-law's chest. Too bad, he would pay the price, but he didn't notice at the moment that he was perhaps out of the way from Palace intrigue, a good thing for him. He liked it better that way, she thought, anyhow, and now had a wife, for all intents and purposes. Almere smirked. Mariette glared at her. Tevron looked pale; his breathing was slow and then rapid; he appeared dizzy and disoriented.

"Confused?" Almere asked. He stammered.

"I d-don't know."

"Did Mariette tell you the incantation to make the dragon charm do its magic?"

"No," he said. "She didn't give it back to me, either."

"I won't, neither." The chubby maidservant stood with arms akimbo, her lips twisted into a sneer. "He left me once. Ain't no way he's going to get away again."

"Good," Almere said. She lifted eyebrows at the couple. "He has a good, strong, and roomy house here in the outback, you know, farm animals and fruit crops. He'd make a good husband."

"No!" Tevron blurted. He turned and ran. Mariette smiled and muttered, touching the amulet around her neck, and disappeared. Two sets of heavy imprints appeared in the soft dark earth.

"Stannock can perform the ceremony," Almere called after them. Branches and twigs snapped from invisible forces and Tevron fell face forward into a patch of mud. An invisible weight settled on his back. Then he was plucked forcibly upwards and set on his feet. A red lip-shaped stain appeared on his cheek. A massive, invisible hug folded his silver shirt and creased the sleeves. He was lifted bodily off the ground and set down again on a little grassy hillock a few yards away. His tight pants ripped in the crotch. Then Mariette reappeared, beaming.

"Give me back my amulet," he gasped, panting.

"No way," she said. "Until you marry me."

"Is that a proposal?" Almere smirked. The dark little jerk had it coming. In the clearing behind her, the dragon brayed. King Stannock's wife needed her husband so that he could preside over what looked like a less than amicable wedding. *But beggars can't be choosers,* she thought, from a dragon's epic poetry point of view. With both of them out of the way and settled in this no man's land permanently, the kingdom would be a safer and more pleasant place to live and reign. She would do it.

"Fire-Smasher," she said, "let's go."

"No!" cried Tevron and took to his heels across the hills, Mariette in close pursuit. Suddenly, she was no longer there, but Almere could see her brother-in-law waving his arms above his head, his trousers around his knees, and one boot in the bog of another puddle. *That should slow him down,* she thought and grinned.

Her husband would be crowned by the triumvirate later that week. In the meantime, he had a professional duty to perform as interim king, while the old King Hakor played in his bedchamber with children's toys and tried to remember who that tall woman was, the one in the next bed, who called herself his wife. Somehow, that seemed wrong, but he couldn't put his finger on it. He chattered and grinned and drooled, and when his sons declared him incompetent to the people of his realm and removed him from office, there was no real objection.

Except for Mariette, who loved her monarch well. Not as well as she loved his stepson, but well, just the same. Mariette was a stubborn woman and, when she put her mind to something, was a dragon herself in accomplishing her goals. She had long ago given her allegiance to King Hakor, and never would she give that up for a young upstart like King Stannock. But Stannock did have a studly brother, and the new king wed Mariette and Tevron together the next day in the grove of Thurtle trees and flowering shrubs. As Mariette said to her new neighbors that evening, "THE PISTOL IS NO LONGER COCKED."

She was too old to have children, but adoption would be nice. Tevron was finally and thoroughly caught.

A small black bird with a purple breast sat on a branch and listened, its head tilted, before it flew away.

Chapter Seventeen

"You're Queen Mother now, and Mistress of Dragons," Almere said. "Enough to keep you busy, Ericaania. Can you stop harping on the heirs? Maybe Tevron—" She stopped and smiled because she had a secret.

"Nonsense." Ericaania snapped off her white gloves and inspected her nails. She lifted a cup of wine to her lips. "Tevron's married to that common maid, and she's too old to have babies. I have a dragon for Tevron, my wedding gift to them, a fierce beast from the front lines who was first to deliver the boiling oil to the Picts and Trolls, other than my stout Lockjaw, that is. The King gets to name him."

"Why not Tevron?"

"I'm sending him with my love to Malcoom's son, and he needs a name that the soldiers, crude as they are, haven't given him."

"What do the soldiers call this beast?"

"You wouldn't want to know." Ericaania threw her gloves in the air then caught them. "They're very rude."

"Where is this beast?" Almere raised her pretty eyebrows.

"At the front lines, as I said, and in the general's care, who oversees the battalion that's still keeping peace in Stannock's sector."

"As king, Stannock is torn between his court duties here and the duties of a major general in the army," Almere said. "As his wife and queen, I want him here with me. So, what do we do? What did you do, Mother, when your husband was king?"

"Oh, Hakor was crippled and old, as you know, for many recent years, but when he was younger, we flew to the far lands together, lunched together, and he discussed court business with me – those were the happy days. When Malcoom was alive, I doted on *him* day and night and prepared his meals myself. The boys were small then, and kept my maidservants busy, and I took my sons more often than not to the hills and the valleys and showed them our lands. It was a happy time."

"It can be happy times again," Almere said.

"Does Stannock suspect palace intrigue brought him to the front lines with the King's seal on the message? My sons, ever warring with one another."

"Yes, he knows of Tevron's duplicity. That's why he's more or less banished to the badlands, with Mariette who chased him until he caught her." Almere chuckled. "It's the best thing that could have happened to Tevron. The old general, who sent the message, was innocent. He was doing simply as he thought his king directed him to do, though it meant almost certain death for Stannock."

"But Tevron is forgiven?"

"I don't know if Stannock has forgiven his brother, but he understands that Tevron may have been cursed by the swastika cross he wore, and by jealousy and inactivity. As a warrior, Stannock does make allowances for the deception. Stannock has never blamed the general."

"King Hakor never knew of the stolen seal?"

"No, he didn't know that message had been encrypted by his advisor, Tevron, and sent with his servant on my Fire-Smasher to the battle zone. If I hadn't found them where they fell at the cliffs, both would be dead. But I went to the boy first, as a human being, after seeing that my dragon may be mortally wounded. It's something that I regret, for Paige proved rude and deceptive, though loyal to his master."

"His master Tevron? Yes."

"Yes. My dragon lived. Praise the powers of fire that protect all dragons, my Fire-Smasher lived and is thriving, a miracle of bone and muscle and spirit."

"You love that dragon more than you love Stannock, I think," the Queen Mother observed. "That's not right."

"No, no more than I love Stannock, but in a different way, as we love our beasts of the air. He has my soul trapped in his fire. When I ride him, the cares fall away from me and I can think only of the air rushing past my face and his wonderful throbbing form between my legs."

The Queen Mother sniffed. "Hmmm."

Almere smiled to herself and trotted to the cabinet in the corner of the foyer where they talked. The cabinet was white with brass hardware, formed wondrously by the Palace craftsmen, with snakes and toads cavorting down the pillars on each side. She touched a gem in the middle of a toad's forehead and a drawer sprang open, revealing a collection of porcelain dolls and one small porcelain dragon painted in various shades of turquoise and green, like Lockjaw, Ericaania's mount.

"How exquisite!" the old queen exclaimed, scattering the toys on her lap and catching the tiny dragon as she did. "What are these, then? Where did you get them? You know I have a collection of small porcelain pieces, but I've never seen any quite so sturdy or formed for small fingers. Are they for a child?"

"Yes." Almere blushed. "I know how much you want grandchildren and heirs, Mother. Stannock and I – we think perhaps – well, it's too soon to tell, but..."

"Almere!" The older woman clasped the toys with joyous abandon. "I could kiss you, my dear! Come here, let me hug you. But careful, careful, you don't want to hurt yourself – should you be riding now?"

"The King's chief medic lets me ride," Almere said. "He is careful to explain what I may and may not do, and he's very modern, Mother. He said anything within reason. And that exercise and fresh air is good for me and good for the…"

"Oh, don't say the word! The baby! This is such good news. Why didn't Stannock tell me?"

"He thought we two women ought to discuss it," Almere said. "As someone who's had two sons, he thought his mother would be most helpful to me. There's so much I don't know."

"My dear, if only Hakor could know. But he's disappeared into childhood himself, plays all day with his toys, and can't remember my name. It's sad, I've done this to him, but it was necessary. I still love him, you know. But not as I loved Malcoom."

"I know."

"Let's tell him. He's in his own quarters where we've moved him and Jon. He never leaves his rooms anymore. Maybe this will make him happy as I am."

Almere patted her flat stomach. "I think he's happier than he has been for many years. He doesn't have the worries of the court nor the concern that he's carried for years."

"Yes. Let's go tell him now."

Old King Hakor was in his rooms, as they said, with Jon, his manservant, bathing his feet. The old man greeted them. "A baby?" was all he said and went back to staring at the blue sky out the window. "I saw a bird this morning. I think it was a Bobbly, Mother."

"I'm sure it was." The queen mother laid one white hand on Hakor's shoulder. "Do you remember your son, Tevron?" she asked him.

"Tevron. My son?" Was all the old king said before he went back to humming to himself. "Oh, yes. The little boy with the black, black hair. Like that other big man, Mommy, what was his name?"

"Malcoom, dear," she said. "And Tevron is now a man. He has a fierce dragon, from the front lines, and we want to name him before we send him to our son."

"A dragon?"

"Madam," Jon said, straightening from washing Hakor's feet. "May I suggest a name from the Book of Apocalypse? It would seem appropriate in these times." His forehead furrowed and he brooded over the King's jeweled hand. "My liege," he said. "The book?"

He withdrew a battered black Holy Book from Hakor's cabinet, where the poison had been held – still, the queen mother thought, she forgave the old man. He had not been right in his head for many years.

"That's the Old Religion," Almere said. "It has been banned for centuries. But my husband is going to declare now that the Trolls and Picts have a truce with the kingdom, the healers will be allowed in the land again, and they can practice their old religion."

"I was instrumental in that decision," Ericaania said, smacking one hand against the other while she held up the book. "We've been too long in the dark ages and it's time to move forward."

She continued, "I think Azazel is a beautiful name, from the Apocalypse of Abraham, the Old Religion, and nobody can say it was the healers who destroyed the kingdom. Rather, the intrigue that tried to keep us in battle for far too long, the soldiers and civilians, dead and murdered, an atrocity for our Kingdom."

"The Old Religion speaks of love," she continued. "Peace and joy."

"Also, destruction and death," Jon said. He pursed his wrinkled lips. "Kingdoms fallen into dust long ago."

"Long live the new world," Almere said. Jon handed Hakor a towel, with which he dried his feet.

Hakor frowned, trying to remember. "What was it you said?" he said. "A kingdom? What does that have to do with me?"

"Nothing, darling." The old queen withdrew her hand from his shoulder. "Nothing at all. We just wanted to consult you."

"Who are you? Who am I that you want to consult me?"

Jon frowned and wiped a small tear from the corner of his eye. "My liege," he murmured. "You are always the king. I have never acknowledged another."

"Oh, I see," King Hakor struggled with his words. "The little Bobbly, Jon, outside the window there. He sings so well. Let's reward him."

"Yes." Jon reached for a small bowl of seeds they kept for that purpose. "Let's spread the seeds on the sill for him, sire. He'll sing more for us, I think."

"Good," Hakor said. "It's Azazel, then."

Almere's eyebrows shot up. "Thank you."

"Good night, dear," Ericaania said. She and Almere brushed through the heavy tapestries at the front of the room on their way out. "I didn't think he knew what we were talking about."

"That's our king," Almere said. "He surprises us all."

"Yes, he always has," Ericaania agreed. "Usually in a bad way."

"This isn't bad, Mother. This is the beginning of something great. A new kingdom and a new heir."

"A mount for my wayward son, and a wife for him. A court appointment. I hope Tevron's satisfied with that."

"I'm not sure what he'll think of the heir," murmured Almere. "He thinks he's next in line."

"That's why we want him far away and under Mariette's thumb," the queen mother said. "He could be dangerous."

"Indeed, he has proven so," Almere said. "Much like the old king, whose power went to his head."

"Power does that. But it's not power that corrupts, it's the man."

"Or woman," mused Almere, patting her tummy. "It could be a girl."

"All the same," Ericaania said, "We must be careful of the green-eyed monster. I don't mean the dragon, either."

"I know. Jealousy."

Stannock remained in the badlands, whittling small swords and dragons out of wood scraps in his spare time when his men were bivouacked and he was alone. There would be gold for his queen, lush silken garments from across the Agave Sea, fruits and sweetmeats in abundance, and he would see to it that she rested, away from Fire-Smasher and her court duties, for this would be his son and the new heir to the Kingdom of Gracklen. Stannock was content.

Many leagues away in the settlements, his brother rested in Mariette's arms, the amulet around his hairy neck. The amulet seemed to squirm above his heart, in the wiry black chest hairs, into the soul of treachery and indifference to love.

Chapter Eighteen

The wrinkled old woman sat on her blanket surrounded by brilliant gemstones and jewelry from all corners of the Agave Sea and the lands beyond Gracklen. The blanket was old, too, with broad black and red stripes. Surrounded by Draxxt's equivalent of agates, pearls, moonstones, turquoise, jade, and silver, the old woman peered from behind hooded eyes at the tall figure standing in front of her, not knowing it was her new queen who asked for her help.

"Fertility?" she croaked. "The finest moonstones here in a bracelet, my lady, for a modest price." She gazed to the heavens and uttered a charmed word. "The moonstone, like on the old world from which we all traveled millennia ago, my lady, is a charm against infertility. It's what you want, I think, this bracelet, clasped with pearls, and studded with fire jewels from mines deep underground, from our Armgado mines and further away. Only the Trolls knew of its power and charm, until now, when we are one with the Kingdom of Gracklen and the badlands. Long live the King."

"Yes, our land is free and we're free to follow our faith in this country now," Almere agreed. "You're quite right. We have a good and just king." She wondered what the old woman really thought of this new ruler, or if she were simply being cautious with a stranger, not knowing whether she should divulge her true feelings. Was Stannock loved?

"It's a blessing I've lived long enough to see our new kingdom. I'm a healer, madam, and no longer have to hide. These are my wares, magic in them and charms, and if you're not afraid of the old magic, then sit down and see what I have to offer."

"You're so open," Almere marveled. "Is this really what my husband has done for the country?"

"Your husband?" The old healer grasped a shiny bracelet in one gnarled hand, fingers shaking. "You flatter yourself, madam, though you have the bearing of a queen. But news travels fast here in Gracklen, even in the badlands and the outback. We know of the new king and that he has a young wife. We know also that his half-brother hides here in the land of Many Waters, with a mysterious woman and a curse on him. Would you be related to that brother?"

"I may be the Queen," Almere said and knelt beside the old woman. "That man you speak of may be my brother-in-law and is harmless. Even now, he and his wife are planning to help the orphans in the badlands, left by the war that killed so many of our people, the Picts, and the Trolls. Mindbender, the King of the Trolls, is healing in the land of Many Waters, near where the King's step-brother wishes to set up an orphanage. You hear wrong, old woman. The King's brother is a good man."

She hoped she was right.

"As you say." The old woman nodded. "You could be Queen or you could not, it's all the same to me at my age. I've seen many marvels, madam, not the least of which is a queen. Which do you choose, then?" the healer asked. "The bracelet will look beautiful on that tanned slim wrist, Your Highness, if that's who you are. I'll throw in a piece of jade as well, straight from the Armgado mines nearby."

"No need to flatter me further," Almere laughed. "But yes, I'll take the moonstones and jade, and a silver chain and black coral for my husband."

"Perfect," the healer croaked and settled the stones into a small pouch. She held out her gnarled hand. "Six thousand lira, madam, and you have a bargain, too."

"Six thousand is the price I'd pay for my dragon's young," Almere scoffed, prepared to bargain. "It's too much, old woman. Take four."

"Five thousand," she croaked, "and a guarantee of fertility and prevention from harm of the baby."

"I'm worried about miscarriage," Almere admitted.

"Oh, then, why didn't you say so, lovey? Here, a piece of aquamarine for your pocket will discourage miscarriage. I'll even give it to you, free, no charge, with the jade. Good luck to you and your husband."

Almere parted the folds of Stannock's tent. Almost bashfully, before their lovemaking, she placed the black coral around his manly neck.

"What is this, then?" he asked. The candles sputtered in their basins on the table in the corner of his tent. His wife slipped the moonstone bracelet around her slim wrist. She crossed to the table and blew out the candles.

"A charm," she said simply.

"The Old Religion rises from its crypt," Stannock murmured. "Where did you get these charms, and what do they do?"

"From a healer," she said. "Outside these walls. We've made a baby together, my husband – it *will* happen. Just as surely as Tevron is out of the way and will leave no descendants, so we will leave heirs."

Stannock laughed and reached for her, drawing her to his chest as he pulled the leathern cords from his trousers to loosen them. "Come here, Peaches," he said. "I don't know about the healers, but they are thick in the settlements here, and you know, don't you, that every charm has a curse?"

"Not this one," she murmured and put her soft wet mouth to his. They kissed long and hard, and then Stannock fell on her, on the infamous cot, and they were lost in lovemaking and each other's arms.

On their journey home, Almere and Fire-Smasher rose and swirled in the currents of air over the Armgado mines but stayed away from the Marlbrex cliffs. They courted and sang.

Stannock stayed behind in his tent, dreaming of his lover, his wife, his soulmate and confidante, and, he was sure, the mother of his future heirs. The black coral seemed to twist around his neck, and he felt a piercing of his heart, which cried out for Almere and the future of his kingdom.

Chapter Nineteen

The planet Draxxt orbited three stars, unlike their ancient Earth birthplace, and four moons clustered in the night sky. It was a rogue exoplanet, unlike Earth, yet strikingly similar in its geology of alien formations and life, a potential and habitable home targeted by humans who left their planet behind in search of safety and peace. Their first tantalizing glimpses of this world, potentially perfect for life, were critical for ascertaining whether it would be home to the weary cosmic wanderers. It lay in the habitable zone of its parent stars.

Draxxt spun close to a cosmic firestorm, almost lost in the flare of its suns. A hundred billion years ago it formed as a gas giant. Its gaseous shell blasted off into space, revealing a rocky core. Machine-gunned by deadly cosmic rays, this tiny orb was once a hostile world cooked by radiation. The opposite hell, frozen worlds too cold for life, were found in the same star system and rejected by the first human explorers. But Draxxt evolved, and the ancestors of the humans on this perfect planet possessed the technology to discover its secrets.

Draxxt trapped enough heat to have clouds, rain, and oceans. It was the closest they had come to a planet like Earth. They found life there, sentient beasts much like the dragons of Earth mythology; they tamed them and rode them and gradually tamed the planet. Their biological experiments produced painted manlike beings they called Picts, and huge Trolls, all from the legends of Earth. Pushing these beings to the fringes of their planet, the humans settled the friendly land in an uneasy truce with their creations. Wars and rumors of wars destroyed the technology which had brought them through the stars. They formed kingships based on the old religion, which almost destroyed them, and eventually the old ways were declared illegal. The witchcraft and magic they found on the planet Draxxt were also outlawed by a succession of kings and their generals. Humans pushed the Picts and Trolls, first intended to be slaves, to the fringes of the vast sea that stretched in the northwest and the badlands to the north of that.

The kings of Gracklen were inheritors of a world with history stretching back several millennia to the beginning of their sojourn on Draxxt, lost in the mythology they brought with them. The kings of Gracklen had bloodlines almost as long.

Coronation Day rode the waves of excitement throughout the Gracklen kingdom. Stannock adjusted his robes over the chain mail armor he wore, symbolic of his rank as Major General in the King's Army. He had practiced walking while he wore the massive golden crown, studded with precious jewels, and padded with fleece around his brow. The sacred abbey before him was decorated with precious metals and gems, strewn with velvet tapestries. King Hakor, and the Queen Mother Ericaania beside his golden wheelchair, waited with the court inside the abbey for Stannock and his new queen to walk the long crimson carpet to the head of the ancient church. Outside, a vast mob watched the proceedings through the open doors and windows of the abbey. They waited for their new king and queen to appear on the balcony over-looking the vast square.

The populace wasn't disappointed. Like cosmic blowtorches, the castle's dragons exploded with fire. It was the biggest spectacle ever seen of the most colorful procession in their world. Only the very old remembered the previous coronation, that of King Hakor perhaps sixty years ago, as a young man, and his co-ruler King Malcoom, who predeceased him. Vast musical symphonies swelled from the horns and stringed instruments of the royal orchestra. The coronation had been timed to coincide with the three suns together in the afternoon sky, and the first of the white moons began to rise. Solar matter exploded from the surface and shot out into space, lighting the face of the abbey's keeper as he laid his hands on the young Stannock kneeling before him, who took his solemn vows and was crowned King of Gracklen.

Their astronomers had predicted just this, the coincidence of the magnetic field of the first star, Daemon, with the flare that erupted from its neighbors. Gravitational forces evened out, born in cold space, and over millions of years the planet spiraled into its present more stable orbit. In less than a million years, it would be consumed by fire. Its orbit was not considered possible by the early explorers. On Draxxt's surface, the power of the violent suns raced across the desolate badlands and lit up the lush green-gold valleys. A king's coronation seemed part of nature's mysterious forces, this moment awaited and planned for. As the keeper declared, the new king would impose order on chaos, as the immense forces of their stars' gravities combined with the motion of the planet to create a stable, but eccentric, orbit.

"GOD SAVE THE KING!" the keeper of the abbey called, and the music swelled.

"What does that mean?" asked a young lad, jostling for space.

"The King has declared there is freedom of faith and religion," explained a gnarled old woman, crossing herself. "He's given amnesty to the healers and witches, and revived the name of God. I've lived this long, to see this, dragon's fire be praised."

"Then we can be Wicca," cried the healers. "And those who choose can be Christians."

"Yes," the men and women formed a circle. "The Old Religion is back in our land."

Chapter Twenty

Something new and exciting stirred in the outback Tevron had named Peace River. Healed and strong again, the Troll king, Mindbender, wrought his organizational magic on the disparate tribes of Picts and Trolls who remained around the shores of the Agave Sea. Tevron carried the weight of the new king's pleasure on his back as he strove to unite the old enemies of humanity under the new banner of a unified Draxxt. As his wife, Mariette, constantly reminded him, as the King's brother he was next in line to the throne and had a responsibility to sway his brother's authority here where he had the most impact, paving the way for his own succession. They worked tirelessly, he and Mariette, with negotiations and numerous meetings into the starry night of Gracklen, its inside of tents erected on the old battlefields.

They gathered in the orphans from the final war, cared for them and fed them, and found their relatives if they could. Tevron helped to move new settlers from the badlands in Many Waters to lusher land further inland. The settlers lost their old homes and were not happy, but adjusted. They were helped along by the generous donations of land and food provided by the King's representatives. The new king was fair and just, they decided, and Tevron did his best to further that idea. It was in his best interests to make peace with the citizens of Gracklen who could bear arms against Stannock's army if provoked, setting the new kingdom up for failure. He didn't want to quell a rebellion, and the Picts and Trolls were enough to deal with, let alone the humans along the border here.

After all, it was Tevron's own proposal of uniting the Trolls and Picts along the lands on the border and resettling the humans who lived there on more fertile land. He enjoyed a modest notoriety as Prince of Gracklen, established the hamlet of Peace River, and used his amulet sparingly on occasion to escape his shrewish wife, when his home life became too tiresome for his free spirit.

Mariette knew his subterfuge with the amulet and made his life a hell at times, even to the point of wrestling with him on occasion to wrest it from him, or to creep up on him in their marriage bed to snatch the precious charm from his chest.

So far, he'd kept it from his overbearing wife. Only her nimbleness in bed kept him by her side at times, and he thought often of Almere and her tanned skin, her bosom partly bared by the gaping bodice she wore, and her black hair and sparkling eyes like sapphires. As Malcoom's son and not Hakor's, he had been passed over for succession to the Gracklen throne.

Brooding on his ill luck one quiet evening, he settled himself on the bank of the river that flowed out to the Agave Sea and saw through the shimmer of invisibility a boat approaching. He knew the oarsmen couldn't see him.

Tevron watched as the oarsmen made land and pulled their boat to dock on the makeshift pier that jutted out into the river. The second sun was setting and only the weakest star remained in the sky, illuminating with its ruby light the figures of the men on the shore and the lone woman who remained in the boat.

She was tall and slim, dressed all in white flowing gowns, with a silver star folded into luxurious sheaths of long blonde hair.

The oarsmen wore green trousers and leather jerkins over green doublets with bells on the bottom. They were small and delicate and wrestled with the boat to bring it close to the dock so the woman could step out. She lifted her skirts, trod lightly on the water, and sprang onto the rough wood of the pier.

What's this? Prince Tevron strained to hear the light chatter of the party on the shore as they made their way toward him.

"As our envoy, Lady, you'll ride the dragon Starbuster to the Palace tonight. We don't have time to spare."

Her voice answered, tinkling like bells to Tevron's ear unaccustomed to Fairy prattle. "Why is she invisible then, my dragon? I don't see her nor do I hear the beat of wings in the evening sky, such as we heard last night on the opposite shore."

"Nay, lady, the talisman is there, on the bank, with the dark, brooding man who thinks he can't be seen."

The vision laughed, and the tinkling continued, coming closer now. Tevron began to sweat. He muttered the incantation again, and his form wavered. Then, inexplicably, he burst into view, even to himself.

"Damnation," he swore. "You can see me?"

"But of course," the Fairy replied. "You have my charm, rough human."

"This is mine." Tevron lumbered to his feet, his pride forgotten, his feet slipping in the mud. "My father gave it to me as a child."

"The Picts stole it from our land," the woman in the white gown told him. "We've been searching for it ever since, and only yesterday we heard of the new king, and his brother who can hide himself at will, the curse on the cross, and the old religion which is new again. I've come to claim what is ours, then we'll be gone, back to our land across the sea."

"It was never safe for you here," Tevron said. "The Fairies aren't welcome here, on pain of death."

"That was the old law," the lady replied. "Your brother has declared freedom of religion."

"How do you know so much?" Tevron turned and ran, then tripped and sprawled across the ground. The Fairy spread translucent wings and fluttered above the ground where he lay, face down in the mud.

"Give it to me." Her kind face burned like a candle. The Elves with her joined hands and surrounded Tevron. He sat up, covered with muck and debris, and clutched the talisman at his throat.

"Never!" he cried.

"Then I shall have to punish you." The star in her hair glimmered and shone. "Come here, naughty man. I've had enough of humans and their greed, stealing what doesn't belong to them and telling sad stories about their bad fortune."

"Who are you?" Tevron asked, muttering again the incantation, to no avail. His form became translucent and shimmered to his eyes, but the Fairy and her company looked right at him as though he hadn't uttered the charm at all.

"I thought you said the Picts took it," he said.

"You humans don't acknowledge it, but the Picts are as human as you," she replied. "They come from the same stock, long ago, from the ship that brought the barbarians to this fair planet, to plunder and kill as you have. They began to paint themselves to distinguish themselves from the palace dwellers and the humans who killed the healers and those who were different, as the Picts were, and the Trolls."

"Wait a minute," Tevron said. "Are you saying the Picts and Trolls are the same as us?"

"The same as you," she said. "We are the natural inhabitants of this world, which you call Draxxt, and we call Minth."

The Prince of Gracklen blanched. "But those are old wives' tales. Go away, raise your sails."

"Are they?" She laughed that tinkling laugh again. "My Elves here would tell you differently. Do you dare to rhyme the curse away?"

"I've heard you can." He tore his eyes from her magnetic gaze and drew his sword. "I dare you to come closer, Fairy Queen, or I'll run you through right clean."

The Elves all chuckled. "Good try," they piped in their high-pitched voices. "Now give us the cross."

"It belongs to no one," Tevron said and tore it from his neck, then threw it as hard as he could, with his rock-hard arm, into the sea beyond.

"No!"

"I'm rid of the accursed thing," he said, "and so are you. I've done a good deed tonight, by sinking that dragon's charm into the sea. It's brought me no end of trouble."

In the darkening water, where the charm bobbed, the sea bubbled and foamed. A great fish leaped from the froth and swallowed it.

"That's my Brown Fish of the Muirs," the Fairy said. "Protector of talismans and me, as his queen."

"I've heard of it," Tevron said. "A wild fish who drowns fishermen on the bank if they're unwary."

"A great service he's done us." The Fairy leaned down from hovering above the rocks on the shore to fetch the talisman from the great fish's mouth. "Thank you," she said sweetly and smiled, revealing sharp pointed white teeth and a forked pink tongue. Tevron shuddered.

"Now go home to your wife and no more games," the Fairy said as she and her Elves leaped back into the boat.

"How do you know all this?" Tevron was brave to ask but, bereft of the swastika cross he had worn since boyhood, he felt betrayed and without protection. He had only recently realized the true power of the talisman, and now it was gone. He wanted to cry, but grown men didn't cry, and this Fairy was departing without explanation. He would probably never see her again. Tevron struck his hand with his fist and roared into the black night. "Give me back my property! It's mine and you have no right."

The boat pushed out into a mist that swirled around the pier. The Fairy and her Elves disappeared into the fog.

He heard her call, as tinkling bells, into the night that was suddenly bright with the last of the moons coming up. "I know everything in the kingdom, human. Because this kingdom has always been mine."

Then she was gone.

Chapter Twenty-One

"King Hakor is the only father you knew," Queen Ericaania said to her son Tevron as she poured them both a glass of ruby wine. "And a poor father he was. He tolerated you only for fear of me and the secrets I held against him, that he murdered my poor Malcoom, your true father, in his bed when you were only four years of age, and Stannock, his son, watched with you, at the tender age of two. It was dreadful. I never forgave him, but I lived in fear of his temper toward you and myself. Malcoom was my own true love, he knew it, and was jealous to the point of insanity. Why he married me after Malcoom, I don't know. Why I married him? To consolidate the kingdom; I needed his bloodline and his power. A very poor decision on my part, but based on practicality at the time. After all, in the new religion it was perfectly legal to take two husbands. Or more, if I'd chosen, as female head of the royal family of Gracklen. I'm sorry, Tevron. You suffered and, if it hadn't been for you and the birth of Stannock, I might have killed the King or killed myself."

Tevron hunched over his cup of wine, deep in the bowels of the Royal Palace of Gracklen, where he and his mother shared a meal of roasted beast and herbs, and he poured out his misery to her. "My father Malcoom was well loved by his people," he said. "I do remember a tall, dark man with a beard, who used to hoist me on his shoulders."

"Yes, but he wasn't that tall," Ericaania laughed. "He seemed tall to you, my son, a little boy who came up to his knees. You resemble him in many ways, though your hands aren't so dainty. Yes, he was loved by his subjects, who knew only that he died suddenly in our rooms one night and was buried with suitable pomp and honor, in a closed coffin. No one questioned it in those days. Gold and lira changed hands, servants were removed, and it was explained that he'd had a terrible accident with a flame while cooking a beast and disfigured his face, killing himself in the process with a spear from the spit that had become dislodged."

"I would have questioned it, Mother." Tevron tore off a chunk of bread with his teeth and chewed.

"You would have had you been older, dear, but you and Stannock were only infants. You don't remember, I am glad, the night that Hakor drew his sword and hacked poor Malcoom's head from his body while he lay in bed. A cowardly, craven thing to do, to attack an unarmed man in his own bed, but Hakor was crazy with jealousy. He let me live through his love of me, and he let you live because I struck a bargain with him not to divulge his terrible secret if he would spare you, my son. I think at the time he might have run his sword through his own son, Stannock, if I hadn't intervened, he was that mad with rage and jealousy."

"What brought him to that point?" Tevron asked. "Though he was always a man of towering rages. I can imagine how that would have happened if you had paid more attention to my father than he felt he deserved."

"Yes, it was my fault, partially. I favored Malcoom, as the first and most beloved man in my life. When Hakor came begging me to marry him, I left my marriage bed still warm when I took him into his own, but ever after I shared Malcoom's bedchamber and not Hakor's. He lived in the next quarter as he does now, and visited me and I him, on occasion. Long enough to beget your brother, Stannock, so I don't regret it. I love Stannock dearly and he is a good man. But you were neglected, my son, and grew up not knowing a father's love. I'm truly sorry."

Tevron tore off a piece of the roast beast with his hands and dipped a piece of the bread into the fragrant juices. He swallowed a draft of wine and sneered. "I hate him, Mother, old King Hakor. I never knew my father, it's true, I remember only bits and snatches of him and that he had a soft and deep voice, used to sing songs and tell stories before bedtime. And I remember that he was often gone to the badlands."

"Yes, I know that King Hakor hoped he'd die on the battlefields, before the peace that lasted until his death. It's over now. There's nothing more to be said. You were left fatherless but alive, and for that I'm grateful."

"I'm grateful, too, Mother. Thank you for saving me. It hasn't been easy all these years, but it's better now."

"I think Mariette gives you stability and the orphaned children give you something to care for beyond yourselves."

"I think you're right. Certainly, the little ones are a joy to have around. I wish we could have our own, but Mariette is past the age of childbearing."

"I've often wondered what you see in her. I know it's none of my business, but she pursued you until she caught you, and then you capitulated and married the maid. Why was that?"

"I just couldn't stand my ground," Tevron admitted. "She was too strong for me, and she used the talisman against me. It turned to be a curse rather than a blessing, and the more we used it, the more powerful it became. I swear I could feel it twist in my grasp. But I don't regret it. Mariette settled me and gave me a home, with the children, all twenty of them, skipping and crying and shouting in and out of our building.

Good thing we live in the country where space is unlimited, and the house I built with my own hands is good, strong, and spacious."

"Do you have enough to eat, all of you? Enough food, enough wine, clothes enough? I can help."

"No, my brother supplies us with a good salary and gold enough to keep up the orphanage, such as it is, in our own home. I don't want for anything, nor do Mariette or the children. I think he's happy to do it, to keep me away from the Palace and the intrigue here, that has always been a part of our blood."

The Queen Mother leaned closer to her dark and intense son. "Are you happy?"

He thought some more. "I think so, Mother. Yes, I'm happy. Happy is any man who escapes death."

"But truly, Son?"

"I am," he said. "With Stannock in place and my own place secured in the succession, I have a future. My only regret is I'll never have heirs. I've considered adopting a couple of fine lads we are helping to raise, whose parents were killed in the final battle with the Picts and Trolls. They're happy at Peace River, too, I couldn't do more for them if they were my own, but I'd like to adopt the older lads, Mother. Perhaps that would secure my place in the kingdom, as well."

"Always plotting and planning for your own advancement," the Queen Mother sighed. "When will it end? Adopt if you must, but let it be for the love of the boys and not for any personal gain."

"I've fought long enough for my place in the kingdom." Tevron planted his fists on the sides of his silver platter and rose. "I love the lads, I truly do, Mother, but love for me is struck through with expediency."

"Then you'll be disappointed in life," his Mother warned. "As I'm disappointed in you."

"Do you know something I don't?" Tevron's sudden change of heart startled the Queen Mother, and she put one hand to her throat. "Do you think my brother is plotting against me?"

"Of course not. What gives you that idea? I just don't want you to be disappointed. Things don't always work out the way we planned."

"It's the succession, isn't it? It's not secure?"

"Stannock and Almere are young. I wouldn't put my faith in a possible succession, nor rule out the thought of an heir or heirs."

"You know something I don't, Mother." Tevron got to his feet and tucked his silver shirt into the waistband of his black pants. "I've worked and plotted all these years for one thing. The kingship, which should be rightfully mine as firstborn."

"Firstborn to another king," she reminded him. "I don't know what to say to you, my son. You have indeed got the short end of the branch."

"Yes, I have," he almost shouted at her. "I do what I must for Mariette and myself, and the lads and lasses under our care. Other than that, my ambition is what it's always been."

"Time to temper it somewhat, dear," his mother said. "Almere and Stannock are with child."

"What? Impossible! The witch is barren."

"No, she's not, and she at this moment carries the new heir to the kingdom."

Tevron's eyes glossed with tears. "I won't have it!" he shouted and stormed from the room.

At the door, he met Jon coming through with a meal for the disabled king. "Out of my way, old man." Tevron pushed past him.

"What is it, madam?" Jon asked. "Did I do something wrong?"

"No, Jon," the older woman said. "You were in the way, that's all. You work for a man he hates, and he hates everyone and everything at this moment."

"Yes, madam," Jon said, not understanding. "The old king is ailing, madam. I brought him some soup and a loaf of fresh bread with ginger tea, in the hopes of perking up his appetite."

"He's ailing, you say?" The old queen's mouth twisted and she barked like a dog. "Who's not ailing today? I fear for my sons, Jon."

"What is it?" he asked. "Is there anything I can do, or the old king?"

"You're in the service of a child," Ericaania reminded the manservant. "There's nothing he can do that he hasn't done already to the damage of our kingdom."

"Indeed," Jon said. "I don't share your pessimistic view. My liege has always been a kind and strong master to me."

Ericaania tossed a strand of greying hair from her broad white forehead. Her hazel eyes bored into his watery yellow orbs. "You are faithful and good, Jon. I appreciate you and so does our liege, I know, though he hasn't shown it all these years. Now it's impossible for him to remember his own wife's name, let alone yours. But go your way." She put a pale hand to his cheek. "You are a good man. Take care of his Highness. I loved him once. Maybe I still do."

"I'm sure you do, Madam. How could you not?" He pushed past her with the steaming platter of soup, bread, and tea in his arms.

"Do you remember Malcoom, Jon?"

"Yes, madam. I remember the good young king."

"Good." She stood by the table so recently vacated by her firstborn son. The remains of their meal lay scattered on the floor, where he had pushed it in his haste to get out of the room. *He is not a king-like man but is more like Hakor than Malcoom. What have I done?*

Remembering Tevron's subterfuge with the King's seal, she feared for Almere and Stannock and their unborn infant. If it was a son, he would be in danger. She sighed. Always intrigue in the Palace. There seemed no way to get around it.

She didn't know of the Fairy Queen or the loss of Tevron's charm, but its curse followed him now into the Palace of Gracklen even though it was back with its rightful owner, the Fairy. Or perhaps it was Tevron's own nature that cursed him. The Queen Mother sighed again. She must speak to Stannock. She poured herself a cup of wine.

Chapter Twenty-Two

The Dragons' Court convened monthly in their great hall beneath the stables of the Palace, where the four moons shone through slits in the ceiling and a great fire roared in the grate. Lockjaw intermittently replenished the flames with bursts of fire and smoke from his own great nostrils. Their thick hides were impervious to the cold, still, the dragons welcomed the friendliness and comradeship symbolized by fire.

Moonraker, as a bachelor beast, counted the sacks of gold coins stacked near the fireplace, rewards for foraging in man's forests and foreign castles beyond Gracklen's walls. Dragons love gold, especially Moonraker, who had no mate to keep him warm. The crisp snap of gold coins through his fingers replaced any kind of love he might have cherished from a mate.

"Yes, the fairies have returned, and with them, coy magic," Lockjaw rumbled. "Stannock, new King of Gracklen, gave amnesty to the Old Religion, to the healers and witches, so that the fairies feel safe to come to our shores once more. What are we to do? They took the charm of invisibility and with it the curse."

"That's a good thing, dear." Faerydust sent periwinkle and golden scales tinkling through the air. "I'm worried, though, about the gems that our Queen has purchased from the old witch in the marketplace. They will make her fertile, but what will be the outcome?"

"The fairies are mischievous, and their magic unpredictable," Lockjaw continued. "The humans need an heir, and we all know the new Queen will be a good mother, her husband will be a good father, and we'll be ruled like in the old times, benevolently and fairly. That can only be good."

"That's not the matter this Court is concerned with," Moonraker piped up from his corner, scattering gold dust. "There's a new dragon in our fold." They all turned to look at the Fairy's mount, proud and beautiful, in the back of the hall.

"Starbuster," Lockjaw called. "Come forth and explain yourself."

"No explanations are necessary," Faerydust murmured. "She is beautiful and welcome here until her mistress takes her back."

"We don't know what spells the Fairy Queen put on her dragon," a young dragon called from the middle of the room. "She may be dangerous."

"Nonsense, dear," Faerydust scoffed. "We need our females desperately, and she's already mated with our Moonraker, hasn't she?"

Moonraker ducked his great head and nodded. "It happened last night when the moons were full," he said. "But we took precautions, she swallowed the Hemgrate leaf before we mated, and no issue will come forth, I'm sure of it."

"We're not worried about that, though a foreign infant in our ranks might be divisive," Lockjaw said. "The fact is, she belongs to the Fairies, and they'll come back for her, maybe blaming us for taking her into our ranks. What do you say, Starbuster? Did you choose to stay with our Court, and what would your mistress the Fairy

Queen say if you stayed here with Moonraker, our handsome bachelor?"

Starbuster padded on dainty feet to the front of the great hall. She held her head high in the air, rose colored scales cascading down a silver neck. All who saw her gasped at her beauty. Moonraker sighed and rolled his emerald eyes, like gems, to the ceiling of the smoky room. "I'll go with her," he announced. "It's best she return to her home."

"What do *you* say?" Lockjaw addressed the Fairy dragon.

"Wellll," she breathed, "I do miss my home across the Agave Sea. It's lovely there, and the Fairies swirl in colored lace and webbed wings like little insects all day long. At night we dance and sing, all night, until dawn, and then sleep until noon."

"It sounds good." Moonraker dropped the sacks of gold coins he was counting and strode across the room. He stood next to Starbuster, a great behemoth of a dragon who dwarfed the lithesome Fairy mount. "It will solve a lot of problems if I went with her."

"I have a confession." Starbuster dropped her head, not proud anymore. "Moonraker, there are no dragon males or children left in our land of Fairies. I'm one of the few females, and the only male is old and not interested in procreating. I tricked you, dear. I didn't chew the Hemgrate leaf after all. It was a harmless leaf that looked the same. I may be pregnant."

"My dear," Moonraker cried. "It's settled then. I'll go with you."

"Across the Agave Sea?" she asked. "We'll fly together and the distance will seem short."

"I think," Lockjaw began, not sure what to say at this turn of events. "I think we need children as much as you. Fire-Smasher was the last whelp born to our clan, and he, too, will be looking for a female mate soon. Our clan will die out in a thousand years if we have no fresh blood."

"There is a solution." Faerydust swatted him with her huge tail, scales glistening. "We could swap a few of our males for their females, dear. We could make a trade, across the sea, and if the Fairies are agreeable, it will make our stock that much stronger."

There was a cacophony of different voices from the dragons assembled there.

"The Fairies would have to be consulted."

"I don't trust Fairies."

"The Fairy Queen will be angry."

They spoke of Fairies, and humans who came to Draxxt long ago on fiery spaceships, gods transporting them to Draxxt, fiery metal gods lost now in antiquity, but making it their role to serve humans. Myths abounded around these metal gods, not seen for millennia, but they served Humans well, bringing them to this planet where the humans cared for their dragons like children.

Children. Faerydust curled her massive periwinkle tail around the form of her Fire-Smasher, not a small dragon anymore, but grown, virile and strong. Gold coins chinked through Moonraker's hands. Immense scaly bodies jostled for space as they considered the matters which their leaders presented.

Finally, the beautiful dragon opened her mouth and spewed rainbows into the room. "Stop!" she roared . All voices stilled.

"This is silly. We don't have males. You don't have females. Let's make a journey across the sea to my country. The humans and the Fairies don't have a say in our courts, after all. Do they?"

"No!"

"No!"

"Of course not!"

"Then it's settled," she said, curling her body next to Moonraker. "I'll leave in the morning, with my child's father, and any bachelors here who wish to come with us. When we get to my country, we'll send back the single females who wish to return and take mates here. It'll be a fair and pleasant exchange, I think." She looked lovingly at Moonraker, who wriggled with pleasure.

"How do we know you'll fill your part of the bargain?" asked a brave young dragon. "I'd go if it were up to me."

"You'll have to trust me," the young female said. "As I'll have to trust you, when you get to my country, to settle in and follow our ways."

"What are your ways?"

"I told you some," she said. "We hold court daily, we dance and sing all night, we sleep until noon, and we cavort with the Fairies for the rest of the day. They feed us honey and fermented fruits, and we don't touch the beasts of the valley, but eat only shrubs and plants and leaves, and we are healthy and strong. We've lived for many centuries, millennia, in good health and in good standing with the Fairies, who cherish us as their own children."

"Sounds too good to be true," Moonraker remarked. "I'm in."

"You dear, are too young to go, and we need you here," Faerydust said to Fire-Smasher, sheltering him with her translucent wings.

"I know, Mother," he said. "I don't want to leave my home."

"Good, then that's settled." Lockjaw spread his jaws in an enormous yawn. Smoke trailed from his nostrils. The fire burned low in the grate. Moonraker touched Fire-Smasher's massive scaly side.

"Goodbye, friend," he said.

"Thank you for rescuing me," Fire-Smasher whispered. "I would have died at Marlbrex if it hadn't been for you and my dear lady."

At dawn, Starbuster led a few bold dragons into the turbulent air warmed by the first rising red sun. She crooned a haunting song as they flew like dragonflies across the face of Daemon.

Stannock and Almere watched their dragons leaving. "What is this?" Almere asked, turning the moonstone bracelet on her wrist. "Where are they going?"

"I think," Stannock began, "that it's a new day for all of us. Our dragons, too, must follow their destiny."

"That's the Fairy's mount who led them, if I'm not mistaken. And we're better off, I think, if the Fairies are left alone. Old wives' tales, you know, of mischief and abandon in the glens." The bracelet seemed to twist on her arm of its own accord, moving like a tangled worm. "Tevron met the Fairy Queen, who took his charm and the curse that came with it. What of our fertility charms, dear? Are they cursed, too? What sort of monster will they spawn?"

"Oh, you worry too much, dear." Stannock put a strong arm around his wife. "We live in a free country now."

"Does that mean that we can be Christians now?"

"Yes. The Old Religion is back."

A small black bird flew away, over the sea, to report what it had heard.

Chapter Twenty-Three

The dawn came up like Glory. The second sun, then the third, burst over the peach-pink horizon in the south and east, scattering purple clouds above the line of the Agave Sea. Below, the Fairy boat skimmed over frothing green foam to the country beyond imagination. The Elves who set the sails sang and rowed through the surf that crashed onto the shore of the Land of Fairies. They were met by their ethereal Queen, her white robes blowing about her lithe figure. A hulking passenger rose from the rear of the boat, and the Elves helped him through the surf and to shore. Their task completed, they set to work to haul their little craft up onto the silver beach. The Fairy Queen held out her hand.

"Welcome, Mindbender," she greeted, and her voice rang like tinkling bells in the great Troll's ears, who was used to crude and guttural speech and the tone of soldiers commanding their Pictish armies in the badlands. Lilac colored shrubs and verdant wild grasses whispered along a cobblestone path that led to a towering palace of crystal and pearls. The Troll followed his hostess past the great jeweled doors guarded by gryphons and adorned with golden magical symbols.

Starbuster and her hatchling, Little Hakor slithered with them to the magnificent doors. The dragoness and her whelp soared on webbed colored wings to the top of the crystal palace where they perched and watched the pair below with jeweled eyes. The Fairy Queen smiled and waved imperiously in their direction where they sat like gargoyles on her palace.

"Isn't he magnificent?" the Fairy Queen remarked. "We have a male whelp."

The gestation period had been short and the hatchling grew quickly, as dragons do, its mother Starbuster settling it into a straw lined basket of mother of pearl, fitting for the whelp of a Fairy Queen's dragoness.

"Who is the father?" Mindbender asked. "I thought you had no drakes here."

"He's a fine big bachelor from Gracklen," the Fairy said. "Our dragons have a court of their own, and they decided to exchange mates. They had the approval of their human riders. Isn't that fantastic?"

"I suppose so." Mindbender bent his head and put a finger on the side of his face. "We could use more whelps. Or the humans could."

"What's good for the humans is good for the rest of us," the Fairy chimed, and Mindbender frowned.

"I don't think so," he growled. "I've come to you with a request just about that. The humans grow too pesky, I think, and throw their weight around even more so now that the old king is ill."

"But haven't they negotiated a truce? The new king seems fair."

"Humph." He thumped through the main portals of the crystal palace and through the delicate entry doors. The Fairy Queen smiled.

"You need some dragon milk of kindness," she said.

"Humph. I don't need dragons. They're syco-phants of humans. Doting, useless beasts."

Inside, Mindbender was greeted by Fairy men carrying large bowls of steaming water and hot towels, fragrant oils, and peppermint tea with wild honey. He sat on a carved ebony bench with velvet cushions behind his back and sank his feet into a deep golden bowl of warm wa-ter. A Fairy man removed the magic boots Mind-bender wore and rubbed his feet with oil before scrubbing them.

"Heaven," the Troll sighed, sipping on a cup of tea. "But, Madam, I haven't come all this way to soak my feet. We have matters of State to dis-cuss, which I left behind me in Gracklen but fol-low us here."

"Yes," the Fairy sighed, her words flowing away through the open windows like honey slip-ping from a cup. "The matter of the dark Prince of Gracklen, and his ambitions, and the curse of the charm he wore around his neck since childhood, which rightfully belonged here in the Land of the Fairies."

"I'm afraid the curse remains," Mindbender said. "He's done a good thing by trying to unite the Kingdom of Gracklen with the Picts and Trolls, as I've tried to do since time immemorial. The lands they want to give us are acceptable, rough though they be, and the settlers happy with their greener new home in the land they call Peace River, flowing into the Agave Sea. But his ambition is for the Crown of Gracklen, which is held by his brother Stannock and his wife Almere. If Prince Tevron is allowed to continue with his course, he'll split the land apart again, as sure as King Hakor held it together with wickedness and force. Stannock is a fair king and just, but he's weak."

"What has this to do with me?" the Fairy asked. "This land is far from the land of men, and the Trolls and Picts are too warlike for my people, who deal in magic and sorcery, not battle and bloodshed."

"Thank you for transporting me this night across the sea." Mindbender dried his feet and put on the silken shoes the dark Fairy man supplied. He finished his tea and honey. "It shows you're willing to negotiate with us, my Lady."

"Come with me to our Council Hall," the Fairy Queen said in little more than a whisper. "We'll talk there, away from the ears of my Fairy men and the Elves."

Mindbender's steps shook the delicate tiles on the sides of the room as he trod behind the Fairy and brushed through the velvet tapestries at the entrance to the Hall.

"Thank you for sending your message with my Harpster bird." The Fairy patted the velvet cushions beside her with a delicate and pale hand. "It flew all night from Many Waters to my shore and delivered its song to me two nights ago. I consulted with my Court. We think the threat of another major war in Gracklen is enough to affect even the Land of Fairies, here on the other side of the sea, especially now that the Old Religion is loosed upon the land, and the people are buying charms from soothsayers and witches which have a curse on them. The changes will uproot all on Draxxt, the planet we call Minth, to the extent that the humans who came to this planet in their flaming iron gods thousands of years ago may have to be sent back again, their dragons stripped of magic, and the Land of the Fairies plunged into darkness once more."

"The darkness of ignorance," Mindbender agreed. "The humans brought knowledge with them, technology that's been lost because our magic was too strong for them, and their iron gods remain hidden behind the rising suns, where they were abandoned and forgotten by the generations of men that came after them, so greedy were they for the gold of the dragons and the power of magic."

"Yes," the Fairy Queen agreed. "Men spoiled the spirits of peace and have upset the balance of nature and power here on our fair planet Minth, but not for long, I think. They have sent to me a dragon whelp who might father, when he's old enough, the prophecy of a Dracaena, a dragon female with human features who will unite all of Minth – Fairies, Elves, Trolls, Picts, dragons, and humans. We've not had any drakes for centuries, and now we have two, the whelp and its father. The Dragon Council has requested some of our dragonesses to mate with, there in the kingdom. What do you say? Should we send them?"

"It would be a convergence of fate if a dragon were to unite the world of Draxxt after all. I know the prophecy and all dragons know of it, but it's thought to be a tale to lull children to sleep with, not a true prophecy."

"It may not be," mused the Queen. "Still, the dark Prince Tevron is a threat, and his dragon Azazel is a fierce fighting dragon from the border wars. If he could summon the Picts and Trolls away from your benevolent and powerful rule, Mindbender, he could lead a war on the Kingdom of Gracklen they've never seen before. He could destroy their mild King Stannock and his wife and start a kingdom unheard of even in the days of the cruel King Hakor. Everything would be affected. The waves of discord would reach even to our shore."

"Why would he do that?" Mindbender asked. "The war is won; he's instrumental in a truce and resettling the disputed lands. He's next in line for the throne of Gracklen. All he has to do is wait for his brother to become restless on the throne, or Queen Almere to join Ericaania with her band of healers and leave the Palace. All that is possible, if he would only wait and see how this all settles out. Is he really that rash?"

"Yes, I'm afraid he is," the Fairy said. She re-arranged the white folds of her gown like spider webs. "He's always been unstable in his ways, knowing he's not the King's true son, yet the oldest, and thus a jealous man and an angry prince bereft of power."

"Still, he's next in line, if he were but patient."

"I'm not so sure of that," the Fairy said. "An old woman, a healer and Wicca witch, has sold her wares to the new young Queen."

"What is it?" Mindbender asked, reaching for a cup of mead that sat at his elbow. He drank deeply.

"A fertility bracelet, and a charm for her husband," the fairy revealed. "I think it's nothing. It has no real power. But still, they are a lusty young couple and perhaps the Queen's barrenness isn't permanent."

"She's obviously trying for an heir," the Troll mused. "I wonder if there's more to it than that?"

"Let's send two trusted dragonesses to the Palace," the Fairy decided. "They'll whisper to the ears of my Harpster bird, who will fly across the sea with news from the Palace for me. I'm worried about the outcome of perhaps a new war that may envelop the whole kingdom, including desolation to our fair and peaceful shores."

"Yes," Mindbender agreed. "The dark Prince Tevron may have information from the Queen Mother, the old King Hakor's wife, childish though Hakor is, stripped of power and impotent. Yet the new Queen Almere listens to her mother-in-law and takes counsel from her. The whole kingdom knows that. I wonder if something has slipped from the lips of the Queen to the ears of her brother-in-law Tevron and that has led him to behave in this fashion?"

"I'm thinking the same," whispered the Fairy Queen. "There may be cause for the kingdom to rejoice, if not for Tevron and the curse of love that's on him."

"I thought that curse had been removed?"

"He is always going to be an angry and vengeful man," the Fairy replied. "It may be in his blood. It may not be a curse. But I have the talisman, and he wants that back. He is greedy for so many things; it must drive him mad to be so useless."

"In every way," laughed the Troll. "Have you met his wife?"

"Yes." The Fairy smiled with amusement. "But together, they've given a home to orphans. Is that the wife's idea, or the Prince's? He's capable of a good deed, unless he has another plan beyond that of the orphanage and helping poor children."

"I don't know." Mindbender swirled the amber liquid in his cup. "I think he may be capable of a good deed. He is not of bad blood. His father, Malcoom, was a good man, and his mother always kind though a healer – she is a witch."

"Aren't we all?" laughed the Fairy, and her voice again sounded like tinkling bluebells in a forest, echoing through the great Hall so that the Troll's heart was warmed. He spread his hands as though to a fire, though none burned in that Hall – the Fairies had no need of fires; their land was warm and temperate.

"They have a book," the Troll said. "I've seen it in the old King's chambers. It's a holy book, and they can now follow the Old Religion. King Stannock has announced an amnesty for all healers and holy people, and for his mother as well."

"Really? I think that is a part of their past that they left behind them thousands of years ago. A religion to live by and metal gods with fire abandoned in a forest. I think they don't know what their Old Religion consists of, struck through with mythology and legends as it is, curses and charms. It sounds very much like what we have now."

"What's old is new again," Mindbender agreed.

"We'll make a gift of two dragonesses to the new King Stannock," the Fairy said. "We'll choose well, Mindbender, someone fertile and young and pleasing to their own dragons, and then we'll wait for the Harpster bird to fly again across the sea and tell me of the Palace gossip."

The great Troll smiled, a hideous sight. "Done. Your new whelp will grow up to father many more drakes, I think, and your dragons will be happy, and happy dragons make for a happy kingdom on Draxxt. The dragons will be united as they used to be, and there'll be commerce between the Land of the Fairies and Gracklen."

"Do we really want that?" mused the Fairy. "Still, times are changing. We must change with them, even the Trolls, Picts and Fairies, or be left behind."

"Yes, and it's all due to the humans. They created us as slaves, millennia ago, and they gave us nothing in return."

"Oh, I don't think so," the Fairy said. "No, I don't think so at all. There's much we've learned from them, and much we can grasp if only we have the – the—"

"…the ovaries to do so." The Troll laughed. The fairy laughed, too.

"I think," she agreed, "the females are the key."

"The dragons believe it's their duty to serve their human masters," Mindbender said. "As the humans came to Draxxt on chariots of fire, so the dragons believe they are gods."

"Draxxt, Minth, what's the difference?" he continued. "You call this planet Minth, which means Peace. It hasn't been truly Minth since the humans came. Call the beast a dragoness or drake; they're still dragons. Call the humans good or bad – they're still a force to be reckoned with, and have changed the course of our planet. Dracaena, if she exists? A powerful prophecy, to unite us so we're truly Minth. But not too much lies in a name."

Outside on their perch, Moonraker nuzzled his mate, and the little hatchling shone in the glare of the triple suns, his scales glittering like fire. Surely, the future lay with the children.

Chapter Twenty-Four

Fifteen orphaned children, Tevron and his wife Mariette, and two wolfdogs shared the large wooden building he'd bought from the landowner after the Troll Wars were settled. As king's advisor, he lived in the midst of the lush grasslands near Many Waters and the Agave Sea, in the area named Peace River. Though he ought to be content, the ambitious prince felt a charmed life had been snatched from him by his younger brother, Stannock, who was now King. Stannock also possessed the lovely Almere, and Tevron had the maid Mariette, chunky and crude, wedded to him because of a charm she had misused in pursuit of the dark prince. Life was easy in the outback. It wasn't that. Tevron was the son of a king, though not the reigning king, and his inheritance had been snatched away from him by Stannock's father. He didn't blame King Hakor, who had murdered Malcoom. He would have done the same. No, he blamed his mother, who had been too weak to insist on her firstborn son's rightful place in the new kingdom.

"Azazel," his dumpy wife mumbled. "What kind of name is that for a dragon?"

"He's a fierce fighting drake," Tevron said. "Snatched from the ranks of the dragons who won the last battle. The old king named him. It's from an ancient holy book he keeps in his rooms, a gift from my mother the healer. They chose a name from the Apocalypse of Abraham."

"That book is banned from our kingdom," Mariette said. "It's not lawful. The old king ought to burn it."

Tevron frowned. "No, we're a free country now, and all the old religions are lawful. My brother said so."

"Your brother. He'll ruin the kingdom."

"It's already ruined with all the wars and the petty fighting of the nobles in Gracklen's courts. Men like Devvid almost destroyed the kingdom."

"I heard the King trusted his captain and was betrayed."

"That's what happened," Tevron said. "The captain's a turncoat."

"Some say he's a hero," Mariette said. "We have a new system now, a new king and queen, and a new chance at honor. Still, I miss the Palace and the old ways. They were good to me there, and it's hard work here, Tev, harder than I'm used to."

"You thought as a prince's wife it would be easier for you, lazy cow. The new kingdom's built on treachery. Now my mother, the hag, tells me I'm not even in line for the Crown. I'm not in line for promotion. I'm in a dead-end job." Tevron sneered as a foul taste invaded his mouth, the bitterness of betrayal. "Is that what you wanted when you chased me and caught me in the bog?"

"What do you mean? If something should happen to Stannock, maybe on the battlefield, maybe a tricky Troll with a knife in the shoulder blades, or Almere, that hoity-toity bitch – well, what then? You're next in line. You could even take Almere for a wife, you son of a dog, that's what you've always wanted, I know. Never mind me, who slaved for you and hid you when it wasn't convenient or safe. Never mind me, but I'd always be the first wife, don't you forget that. I'll make her life a hell if you do that, mark my words."

Tevron shrugged. "It's all the same to me. We have the children now, they don't have parents, we're both fond of them, and for every boy and girl, we get a price on their head from the Palace to look after them. You should be happy about that. It's a living for you, better than taking in washing at the castle."

"I don't do it for gold." Mariette spread her arms wide to welcome a small boy, about four years old, to her ample bosom. "Come here, Timothie Hill. You've been playing all day in the fields, with the dogs and the other children, and you're filthy dirty, and it's almost time for a snack and a drink. What would you like? But first, a good washing. There, that's a good boy."

The child wiped his nose with a dirty hand. "I don't need to wash," he said. "My mother never said I had to wash."

Mariette frowned. "Your mommy isn't here. She's gone with the Gods to the high Palace in the sky, and she won't be back until the spring." It was the story she told all the children, who had seen their parents run through with swords and burned with fire and were forever scarred.

"Okay," he said. "Just this time," and he allowed Mariette to take a clean rag and dip it into a basin of warm water and wash his face and hands. "Can I have a sugar loaf? Pwease?"

"Yes, you may," Tevron said. "Now go fetch the other kiddies. It's almost time for your nap, after the treat."

"And it's almost time for the older children to study their lessons," Mariette said.

"Can I come?" Timothie asked, sucking on his sugar loaf and jumping up and down around the large kitchen. "Can my baby sister come, too? Pwease?"

"No, not today," Mariette said, pressing her lips together. Tevron brought the books from the cupboard in the corner and set out paper, ink, and quills. Children began to drift in from the fields and took their places at the long tables.

"We're going to learn to read." Tevron began the lesson. The smaller children got sugar loafs and settled down in the next room on blankets and mattresses for their nap. A couple of young women from the nearby farms distributed fruit drinks and covered the children with colorful sheets and blankets. They drew the shades over the large open windows and one of the young women chose a stringed instrument and began to strum.

"I'll take over now," a young man said to Tevron. "You're wanted in the fields, Master."

"What is it?" Tevron asked, relieved of his teaching duty for the afternoon and glad of it. Damn his brother's skin.

"It's a Troll," the young man said, taking up a piece of chalk and drawing on a large blackboard behind the desk. "It's the big Troll, with the colored boots. He wants to talk to you."

"Mindbender," muttered the Prince, and he strode out the door, leaving Mariette to stir a huge kettle of vegetable stew over a crackling fire. He took with him the wolfdogs, wagging their tails and barking at his heels. "Take care you don't burn that fresh bread," he called to his wife as he closed the doors.

"Shut up," she said and put the spoon to her mouth.

The small children slept, and the older children studied. They learned of the old ways and the time that humans came to Draxxt in a metal dragon that was like a god, and ever since, their dragons had served them as gods. That was the human point of view, anyway, thought Mariette sourly. *My man is about as much a god as he is a beast, and I don't know of any husband better than him, anyway, unless it's his hoity-toity brother with the new queen. I know he wants to be king. I would be queen then.* Satisfied with that thought, she stirred the broth.

But what if – what if a little prince was born to King Stannock?

No, the bitch was barren.

But what if – the magic that had caused Tevron to marry Mariette would spread to the Palace and cause a miracle? What if a baby was born, a boy? Or even a girl bitch? That couldn't be allowed to happen. It just couldn't. Mariette's husband would never allow it.

Funny, he was acting stranger than usual lately. He'd been to the Palace and talked to his mother.

He don't share with me, Mariette muttered. The stew needed something, maybe salt from the salt mines in Marlbrex. She added a pinch and slurped. Oh, that was better. She figured if Tevron was a prince, she must be a princess. She smiled, content with the thought, and scratched her buttocks with the end of the spoon.

Tevron was gone a long time, talking to that big Troll. It must be State business. She knew he was busy a lot with planning the settlements and distributing land. That was important to the King. Surely the King knew that. Her husband Tevron would be rewarded, eventually, and so would she. They wouldn't live in this godforsaken place forever. Not for long.

The long wooden tables creaked as the children put their books away. They were training the young farm men and women to teach and care for the orphans. That was a good plan. Tevron was quite smart but not as smart as his brother.

Mariette wished she'd gone after Stannock. But Stannock was married already. She would have been second wife. Not good. She heaved the kettle of stew onto the grate and began to dole out the bowls of steaming broth, roots, and herbs, with a dollop of fresh cream and lots of meat from the spit next to it. They ate well, but not as well as they'd eaten in the Palace, and they worked harder here. She could hardly wait until Tevron was called back home. That fire-breathing drake, Azazel, would carry them there if he didn't upset them first, the fierce fighting beast. She didn't trust him.

"Mindbender." Tevron stood in the doorway. "He has news, wife."

"What news would that old Troll have that was of any interest to me?" Mariette asked, a child tugging at her apron. She shooed the little girl away and stood with arms akimbo. "I'm interested, though. He was at the castle with you, wasn't he, not long ago?"

"Yes." Tevron planted his boots on the dirt floor and grinned. "It's good news, actually, Mariette."

"What, something actually put a smile on that face?"

"Never mind," he said and pinched her boob, slapped her butt, and helped himself to a hearty bowl of stew. "I *am* in a good mood. I'm eating this swill."

"Shut up, husband," Mariette said. "What's so funny?"

"Mindbender," Tevron said. "He's been to see the Fairies."

"So?"

"He brought a charm back with him."

His wife settled herself on a rough wooden bench near the grate. The children in the next room didn't hear this exchange, slurped their meal, breaking off crusts of bread and dipping them into the stew.

"What sort of charm?" Mariette asked.

"It's for the dragonesses the Fairies sent back with him."

"What does it do?"

"We can use it." He showed her a handful of herbs. "There's a prophecy of a Dracaena to be born who will unite all of Minth."

"What's Minth?"

"The fairies call Draxxt 'Minth.' It means 'Peace.' It's an ancient term. It's our planet, the Kingdom of Gracklen, the badlands, the Agave Sea, and the lands beyond that we don't know."

"What does that have to do with the Trolls?"

"Mindbender doesn't want the Gracklen countries united. He's for the Trolls and the Picts, and they lost the war, and for now they're satisfied with land we've given them. But not for long. His vision is far-reaching, and he foresees the day when they'll want more and better land; they'll want the Palace and all its goodies. Another battle will be fought, and he thinks with peace and softness in the Palace as it is now, the Trolls and Picts will win."

"That doesn't sound good for us." Mariette shifted in her seat. She picked at a piece of lint on her apron. Her hands were smeared with gravy.

"It is if we're on the right side," Tevron smirked. "I'm in a position to be on the right side, here in the outback, wife. I know things the Palace doesn't know. And I don't have to report everything, do I? My weekly journeys to the Palace on that fierce dragon you dislike so gives me a chance to find out what's going on there, and King Stannock is too interested in bedding Almere to want to bother himself with the wars and the settlement of wars anymore. He's grown soft and lazy, as he always was when his father didn't hound him to the battles."

"Yes, I always thought he was a lazy sot," Mariette said. She patted the bench beside her. "Sit here, husband, and tell me about Mindbender."

"He has a charm from the Fairies to bring peace. They, too, are soft and no lovers of war. As I am not, either. I chose to stay at the Palace and plot intrigue." He laughed at this and glanced at his wife to see how she'd take it.

"I know," she said. "You never did join in battle."

"My dragon is ashamed of me," Tevron admitted. "He hangs his head in the presence of the other fierce drakes. But I won't be soft for long."

"What are you going to do with that handful of useless herbs?" Mariette sniffed.

"It's a gift," he said, "to the Dragon King, Lockjaw, from the Fairy Queen herself, to spread the blanket of peace to the incoming dragonesses from the Land of the Fairies and make peace over all the land."

"How is that going to help us? You're talking nonsense, and I'm not going to sit and listen to it anymore. You're talking about not wanting peace, and then you say you're going to spread peace from those hoity-toity Fairies and that soft-spoken brother in his crystal palace, all love and peace and forgiveness. It makes me sick."

"Me, too." Tevron laughed again and threw the herbs into the air before they settled on the floor.

"Why'd you do that? I thought you said they're a charm."

"They are. They're all the Fairies had, and all the Troll was given. He gave them to me to destroy them," Tevron said.

Mariette moved sideways on the bench to make way for her husband as he sat beside her. "Why didn't he do it himself?"

"Because every charm has a curse on it. He is afraid."

"You're not?" his wife asked.

"I'm a Prince of Gracklen. I'm impervious to the curse."

"I remember the curse that married us," she said. "It wasn't a curse at all."

"Exactly. I'm a prince, and I think I blessed myself, to bring war and pestilence to the land, and wealth and power to myself."

"What makes you think that? Here we are, caring for children and dogs, and stuck in the outback with the Trolls and Picts and farmers. It doesn't look exactly like a blessing, Tev."

"These herbs," he said and grinned, "I'm going to sweep them up and burn them. They bring peace to the dragons and peace to the land. The dragons will never know, and my brother and his wife will never know. My mother might guess, as a healer, but there isn't anything she can do about it."

"And Mindbender was entrusted with the peace of all Draxxt?" Mariette sneered. "I don't think so."

Tevron began to sweep up the dustings and throw them into the fire. "What do you mean?"

"It doesn't sound smart, and the Fairy Queen is smart," Mariette said. "I know I'm not smart, Tevron, but I don't believe you. I don't believe

Mindbender's story. There's something more to it than that."

"They don't bring peace exactly." Tevron brushed the dust off his hands as the green bits of plant flared in the flames. "They make babies who bring peace. We're useless, the older generation. We've shot our load on war and damnation. That's what the Fairies think. That's probably true."

"Dragon babies?"

"Any babies," he said. "Mindbender was supposed to bring them to Stannock and Almere, to ensure an heir."

"She has the moonstone bracelet and he has some kind of talisman around his neck."

Tevron sneered. "It's a useless thing. But my mother told me something disturbing the other day."

"What's that? I can guess. The Queen has Stannock's whelp inside her, right?"

"Yes. They're going to have an heir. We can't allow that, Mariette."

She considered. "So, what are you going to do?"

"Kill it," he said without regret. "Mindbender said if we burn the herbs, they'll have the opposite effect. They're going to kill all the new babies in the land."

Mariette laughed. "I don't trust that big Troll."

Mariette was right. The Fairy Queen wasn't naïve enough to trust Mindbender with the herbs of peace, nor the dragons with the procreation of their kind, without a proviso. She told Mindbender fire would destroy the charm, she guessed the charm would end up in the fire, and that was indeed the only place it would take effect. The smoke of peace and fertility would rise from the flames throughout the kingdom, and Tevron would breathe of it first. The charm had been set free, burning and crackling in the flames of Mariette's kitchen, up the chimney, and over the land. As the blue smoke rose into the air, carried by fair winds eastward and south, a lone red dragon with periwinkle wings gyred and bucked the currents high above, breathing deeply of peace.

Fire-Smasher would carry the message to his mistress, and his mistress to her husband, and her husband to his mother, and his mother to the kingdom. The two lovely dragonesses settled into Lockjaw's clan. It was a time of fecundity throughout Gracklen and beyond, and Almere soon found it impossible to hide her pregnant condition. Was there a curse with the charm?

No one knew, at this point. If there were a curse, it was hidden by great joy as the time of birthings grew near.

Chapter Twenty-Five

The air above Peace River sparkled and smelled oddly, the land of the settlements, north by northwest of the Agave Sea, and home of the dark prince and his wife. Thrown into the cooking fire, the Fairy's herbs curled and sizzled, little bits and white smoke rising from Tevron's chimney.

"I guess I've destroyed that peace charm from the Fairy Queen," Tevron said with a sense of victory. "It's all burned up, just as the big Troll said it would be."

"I guess you might have done the job, all right," Mariette rinsed out the stew pot. "All that la-de-da stuff about peace and hope makes me sick."

"Maybe it's best if they *think* that we're for it, though." Tevron grew thoughtful as he continued to watch the fire burn the dense logs and the last of the herbs vanished into ash. "Put them off guard, I mean."

"It's quite a shock to hear the Queen is pregnant. After all this time. Looks like she's not barren, after all. Bad luck to the rest of us. Stannock's young, younger than you, husband. Even if they don't have an heir, when do you think he'd die and leave the kingdom to you, anyhow? Huh? Ever thought of that?"

Tevron pulled off one of his boots and threw it into a corner. He pulled off the other one, rubbing his feet. "Stannock could die in battle," he said. "Ever thought of that?"

"That didn't work out so well for you, did it? The weakling even forgave you for trying to get him killed. The war's over. How is he going to get killed in battle?"

"The Trolls and Picts aren't settled in their own minds," Tevron plotted, his mind putting the pieces of the dreaded puzzle into place. "They want more land, and Mindbender is greedy. I think he wants the Palace for himself. If I could make a deal with the Troll, and the Troll makes a deal with the Fairy Queen, and Stannock dies, somehow, before the child is born…"

"Somehow. Maybe with some help?"

"The child would still have to die, especially if it's a boy. No, Mariette, that Crown is mine, it's been denied to me, and I will have it." He began whetting his knife on a stone.

"Hmmm. It would be real nice to be queen." Mariette preened and loudly washed the rest of the plates and spoons.

High above Peace River, Red Fire-Smasher breathed deeply of the smoke and the little bits of herb fluttering through the air so high above the settlements. He felt strength and peace in his lungs, and an increased libido in his body stirred his loins. He was coming of age. He recalled some epic poetry his father, Lockjaw, and mother, Faerydust, had taught him as a hatchling and roared through the air:

> 'Your strength surpasses my own,
> For why do you lord like a wild bull
> Over the people of ramparted Uruk?
> Are you not the king,

Shepherd of the people?'
Gilgamesh answered, spoke to Enkidu:
'No one before opposed my strength
Now I have found a worthy companion.
Together we could go to the Cedar Forest.'
Enkidu puzzled said to Gilgamesh:
'Why do you wish to do such a thing?'

Dragons were somewhat telepathic, and Fire-Smasher, though still young, searched with his mind below to the land of the Trolls, by Many Waters, where the Agave Sea drained into a swamp and various tributaries, creating a wetland at Peace River.

"*GILGAMESH.* The two brothers must battle and together defeat the enemies of their kingdom," he said aloud, soaring on translucent periwinkle, emerald, and scarlet wings across the fiery disc of Daemon, the first sun, then banked back and down, surfed through smokey air to the hut where Mindbender nursed his wounded pride. Behind the dragon, a black bird flew, listening.

They both sensed Mindbender's deception, and Tevron's jealousy, and did not trust either of them.

I must go to Queen Almere and tell her of my suspicion.

Tell her what you know, the Harpster bird sang. *I'll tell my Mistress, too. Do you hear the faint but lovely music in the glen from the Land of the Fairies? Do you hear it, mighty dragon?*

Fire-Smasher puffed great clouds of steam and fire, and Mindbender looked up, but the dragon and his escort had left already, like tinder blazing up a chimney on a cold night.

The music of the Fairies reached my ears. What are they celebrating, so far across the sea?

They celebrate life, peace, and love, the Harpster bird sang. *They celebrate the herbs of peace that are wafting over the kingdom.*

They celebrate too soon. But Fire-Smasher felt a great joy in his heart, and the blood pumped through his arteries to his mighty head, fueling fire and smoke from his jaws, and thrusting downward to his loins and the tip of his barbed tail. The Harpster bird flew north to the Land of the Fairies. Fire-Smasher flew southeast to the

King's castle, where Almere turned the moon-stones on her wrist, and her lips turned upward, and the old witch woman in the market strung charms onto thin wires, enticing peasants and royalty alike.

Chapter Twenty-Six

Four moons, each smaller than Earth's moon, lit the glen as though the first and most important sun, Daemon, blazed in the night sky. Beyond them sprinkled stars of such immensity and so numerous that mortals' ancestors, when they landed millennia ago, bowed in awe as they stood in the cinders left by their ship.

In the distance, hedges stood silver against the sky-scraping spires of the Palace. Moss that served as benches lined the clearing. In the center was an Elvish orchestra, who piped on flutes, plucked stringed instruments and danced with magic shoes amongst white daisies sprinkled like stars throughout the soft grasses and reeds. Laughter tinkled into the crystal air, carried far away by soughing breezes across the sea. Fairies danced, male and female together, light as froth on an ocean, whirled in splendor of silver and lilac, delicate wings carrying them across the faces of the yellow moons and down again to the glen.

"We celebrate the herbs of peace wafting over the kingdom," sang the Elves, "We celebrate the prophecy of a Dracaena who will unite the peoples of Minth. We sing because we're happy and loved, and we celebrate our beloved queen. We sing, we sing, we sing and dance because it's the hour of enchantment when all beasts talk and the Fairies play."

The Fairy Queen smiled in her corner, resting on her piece of moss, her wand in her hand, glimmering softly. She lifted her lovely white face to the warm night air and listened. From the star speckled sky flew a black bird with a purple chest.

"Why, it's my Harpster bird," the Queen exclaimed. "Do you have a message for me, darling, or did you simply hear the music and come to join us?"

She listened closely as the bird perched on her shoulder and sang into her ear. She clapped her hands and laughed at what she heard. "Oh, lovely, the new Queen is pregnant! I don't think it has anything to do with that silly moonstone charm she bought from the old healer, either, little bird! Yes, her husband is virile and she has less stress now the final battle is done and the kingdom is at peace. An uneasy peace, a truce, really," she admitted, as the bird continued to sing.

"The big Troll did as I imagined he would do, burned the herbs, the silly beast. Oh, the dark Prince in the settlements burned the herbs? Just the same, the deed is done. That means there is a truce between them, the Troll and the King's brother. Interesting."

"What's that, little songbird?" She strained to hear over the Elvish music and the whir of a myriad of little wings in the air. Only two moons remained in the sky. Shadows danced over the glen, interspersed with silver.

"Oh, no." The Fairy Queen rose. "Tevron his name is, let's call him by his name, a name of deception and treachery, that will be infamous forever in Minth if this deed is done. He wants to kill the King and his royal child? Oh, no, that can't be allowed to happen."

A tear fell from the bird's eye. The Elves quit playing their instruments. The Fairies stopped dancing and cavorting through the air, and the fourth moon set, plunging the glade into semi-darkness lit only by the Queen's shimmering wand and the lights of the Palace beyond the dark hedges.

Fire-Smasher, flying home again, realized he could no longer hear the Fairy celebration. Limited as he was at human speech, he wondered if he could make himself understood to his dear Queen Almere and warn her of what he suspected. Treachery and intrigue in Gracklen always affected the dragons of the kingdom. They were empathic – almost telepathic – and so sensitive to the moods and mysteries of their human companions that their color changed with their riders' emotions. Even the scarlet hues of Fire-Smasher's sides were muted at times by the periwinkle and emerald translucent wings he beat so strongly now that he had matured, and the many moods of his Queen. Now, as the countryside streamed in its verdure beneath him – valleys, mountains, and deserts – he pondered on the iron hand of old King Hakor and whether it had been preferable to the softer approach of his son. Surely the dark prince was more like Hakor than the true son. Fire-Smasher's heart beat with a love for the royal family that he couldn't explain, and he thought his heart would break as the King's guards pulled the chains that allowed him to land in the outer courts.

He met his father, Lockjaw, in the stables, recently back from a ride with the Queen Mother.

It's a quiet day for the king and queen. Lockjaw tasted a new plant that Ericaania had left for him with a small mammal to tempt his palate. He pushed the mammal to his mate, Faerydust, and she nibbled then pushed it back. She rubbed against Lockjaw's huge side, and silvery scales fell like stars. *Thank you,* she thought. *It is a very pleasant small beast. Is there more in the Great Hall, by the fire? By the gold?*

Yes, Lockjaw rumbled, his mind busy with what their son, Fire-Smasher, had told him. *There are more of us to count the gold now. The*

dragonesses settled in well and are making themselves at home. I hear that Moonraker's mate had
a hatchling and they called him Little Hakor. Very
nice. I miss the old king. Our kingdom isn't the
same since he fell ill.

No, dear. Faerydust wandered away. But our
Fire-Smasher loves the new queen. Always has.
They grew up together.

You're right, they did.

Fire-Smasher, miserable, chomped on a pile of
fresh grasses and new growth that the Palace
guards had left for them. The dragons ate
enough on their forays into Gracklen's glens
and valleys but were always voracious and ap-
preciated the meals left for them by the King's
men.

You have to tell them, dear. Faerydust caught
the end of their thoughts and flew back across
the hall. They must know there is treachery in the
kingdom.

There's always been treachery. Lockjaw
opened his great mouth and flames burst
the length of the room. Hakor started it when he
killed his rival and allowed the rival's son to live.
What did he think would come of that?

He made a bargain with his Queen.

Malcoom's son will split the kingdom.

We must tell the Queen.

Which queen, Mother? Fire-Smasher swept his tail along the floor and dribbled sparks from his jaws. *The old queen, who will always be your queen? Or my Almere, the darling of the skies?*

Both. They both must know. You're closer to Almere. You must tell her of your suspicions.

Lockjaw chewed and reared on his great hind legs. *They're only suspicions. He doesn't know.*

Still, Faerydust said, *he must tell her. It's only right.*

I will, the red dragon said. *Tomorrow, when we swirl through their kingdom, we'll talk about it, I promise, Mother and Father. Stannock and Almere plan to visit their settlements and the outback to-morrow, and I will tell them before they see the treacherous Troll and his friend the dark prince. At least they'll be prepared.*

Don't be surprised if they don't believe you, Lockjaw warned. *I hardly believe you myself.*

Now, dear. He's our son. He's young, but he's very bright, and we all have those powers of mind that he picked up on today. The Fairies celebrat-

ing? They must be celebrating peace, and there will be peace on Draxxt.

I AM FATE, roared Lockjaw. *I AM DESTRUC-TION.*

Don't be silly, dear. Faerydust patted her mate on his broad scaly back. *You've been listening to too many ancient stories. They've turned your head.*

Ericaania liked my song, Lockjaw said and snorted, but no fire emerged from his mouth, and he slunk away into a corner and counted the gold.

Chapter Twenty-Seven

By morning the bird was rested from his flight across the sea to the Land of the Fairies, and as he joined his fellows in the Dawn Chorus, he sang of joy. The Fairy Queen listened, attended by her maidens. She thought long and hard about the human kingdom on the other side of the aquamarine waters. She thought of what the Harpster had told her, of the intrigue and treachery and even danger the new king and queen could expect, if they were not warned. Not wanting to become involved in the affairs of the humans, still, the Fairy Queen felt compelled to warn them, if just to keep her own domain safe and the land of Minth well and happy.

The Fairy had lived for eons before the harsh King Hakor ruled. She had seen kingdoms come and go, been untouched, and danced in the moonlight unconcerned about what transpired over the sea. That there was yet another country, a wild place, on the other side of the Agave Sea to the west and south, she knew, but had never ventured there. She thought it a green, wild portion of Minth where the Fairies did not visit nor had they ever seen it, only heard that it may have been the land to which the Trolls fled, long ago. She heard there were castles there, long abandoned, and gold mines the Picts and dragons had exploited, long ago. Lost in the mists of time, she thought and leaned her pretty head on a delicate hand, gazed out a window at the flock of chattering birds, her own Harpster amongst them.

She whistled, tones clear and haunting, and the black bird with the purple breast swooped immediately through the open window and onto her shoulder. It sang an old song. It was an ancient bird, long used to serving the Fairy Queen, as its father had before it.

"Dear Harpster bird, I wish you to fly again across the sparkling turquoise waters beside us, and sing to the new Queen of Gracklen, that she may be warned of the plot you told me of last night."

The bird cocked its head and trilled.

"I know, we have never become involved with the affairs of humans. But this is a potential war that could rend more than one country apart, split it in two. Already there's discontent with the weak new king. Or that's how his subjects perceive him. He ought to take strong measures against his cunning brother and the Trolls, or he'll not live long, nor will his wife and child."

The bird hopped onto a nearby white onyx table and pecked at a sheet of paper. It picked up a quill dipped in ink with its small yellow beak, and flapped over to the Fairy, bright intelligent eyes pleading.

"I see," the Fairy mused, accepting the quill and paper. "I'm to write a note. You're right, little Harpster, I think that Queen Almere would not believe you. It has to be in my own handwriting, with my royal seal, and she'll have to pay attention." She bent to the table to put quill to paper. The bird cheeped. She straightened.

"Of course," she said. "I'll compromise myself by putting this on paper. My royal seal will serve only to identify me to our enemies. So, what am I to do?" She put the pen and paper away and sat some time in thought. The bird sang.

"I'll simply say that you are my envoy, and she is to pay attention and treat you with the respect she would treat me." That decided, the Fairy retrieved the paper and penned a few strokes with the quill, signed it in an elegant hand, and affixed the letter with her royal seal. The bird took the letter in its yellow mouth, swirled around the room a couple of times, dipped its wings in salute, and was gone out the window to the east.

When the Harpster bird arrived at the King's Palace in Gracklen later that afternoon, Almere was sitting in the nursery which the Queen Mother Ericaania had decorated for the upcoming new arrival, the much-anticipated grandchild. As a healer, Ericaania had attempted to know the sex of the child but had been unsuccessful. The ribbon had swung in circles, then in a straight line over the swell of Almere's belly, and the test was inconclusive. Almere sat in the yellow, mint green, and cream colored room where her baby would lie. A beautifully carved wooden cradle stood in the center of the room.

Mariette had sewn a coverlet of white and yellow flowers of the fields to swaddle the baby. There was the usual white and gold furniture, with silk cream sheets and satin pillows. Mosaics of muted dragons and mythical creatures hung on the walls. Perhaps it would be a boy. Stannock would like that. A boy would guarantee the bloodline of another generation to take the throne. But according to the new Constitution of Gracklen, a girl would also inherit the Crown.

So, it didn't matter much to Almere whether she bore a son or daughter, a prince or princess. It mattered to her husband, though, who paced in front of her deciding on names.

"I think Stannock the Second," he said once, and then, "No, I think Prince Hakor, after my father the old king."

"There's a dragon hatchling named Hakor," Almere reminded him.

"Oh, yes." He swore in a low voice. "What about Tevron? My brother might be mollified by having an heir named after him."

"I don't think so," spoke up the clear voice of a creature perched on the casement. "I come from the Fairy Queen to bring you news of your brother and Mindbender, the great Troll. Here is her royal note, sealed with her own wax ring."

"What is this?" Stannock asked, and Almere frowned. "I don't take orders from a bird."

"This is the Fairy Queen's messenger." Almere slit open the document, which was addressed to her, and read quickly. "The note says only we are to respect her Harpster bird and listen as though it were the Fairy herself murmuring into our ears. Because she has news of high importance to the kingdom."

"Go ahead, bird," Stannock said. "But don't be long."

As the bird sang sweetly into Almere's ear, she blanched and then drew back.

"Stannock," she whimpered.

"What, dearest?" he asked, coming to his wife's side in three great strides. "Has the bird upset you, then? What did he say? I can't interpret Fairy voices nor the voices of their – er – familiars, if that's what this creature is."

Almere rose to her feet, upsetting the small table by her side. "Go home, wretched bird! I don't believe you." She flailed her hands at the creature to chase it away. The bird fluttered about the room, flapping one wing and acting as though crippled, dancing on its two strange feet, trying to get attention, all the while crying out its warning that Almere and Stannock refused to heed.

"I'll consult my dragon," Almere cried. "He'll know the truth. He was there just the other day."

"What?" Stannock put a strong arm around his wife's shoulder. "Don't be upset. It's not good for the child."

"This creature tells us of a plot by your brother to kill our child when it's born and to take your place as king, as the elder brother. He says Mindbender is in on the plot, and together they'll banish us, kill the child, and rule."

"I don't believe it, either." Stannock smiled, a cautious expression and an attempt to reassure his wife. "It's a ruse by the Fairies to divide the kingdom."

"Yet it's true, your brother forged the old king's seal and wrote a note for your general that tried to get you killed in battle."

"That's long ago and forgotten now. He wouldn't dare wage war against his king. Even he is not that headstrong and foolish. My army would demolish them both."

The bird sang. Almere put both hands to her ears and closed her eyes. "I don't believe that treachery is coming from within. It comes from across the Agave Sea, if there is treachery, and jealousy of a land that is now peaceful for the first time in centuries."

"Yes," Stannock said, but he bit his lip and frowned.

"What is it, husband?"

"Nothing," he said. "Just – Tevron has never been close. Could it be possible?"

"There's a mist of peace all over Gracklen," Almere declared. "Your subjects love you and trust you. The old king is indisposed and won't be a bother again. Your mother is happy with her healers and Lockjaw in the valley. We've never been so – so – peaceful." She patted her round belly. "I refuse to believe there's a canker in our midst such as the bird says. The Fairy Queen, also, you'll remember, Stannock, didn't ever write anything about treachery or deception, nor did she speak the name of Tevron. I healed the great Troll myself, and he was most grateful. I don't think any of this is true."

"But what if it is?" Stannock paced, his soft black leather boots whispering on the thick rugs in the nursery where they bantered back and forth, uncertain of their perceptions now that their greatest fear was brought out into the open. He wore a green tunic over tight leggings, and a silver chain with a black coral swung around his corded neck.

"Fire-Smasher was at the settlements just yesterday," Almere said. "He'll know if this is true. He saw Mariette and Tevron and spent most of the day with Tevron's new drake, Azazel. He hasn't said anything to me, his companion. Why would he keep quiet if such a thing is known in the badlands?"

"He wouldn't. He's loyal to you. I know he's young, but he has the same keen empathy that all dragons possess. He'd be able to tell us if something's wrong in the kingdom over there. You're right, sweetness. This bird from the fairies may not be telling us the truth, or the whole truth, or it may be a lie the Fairy Queen has spun to protect her own kingdom, which she may think in jeopardy if Gracklen becomes united, perhaps the land overseas of the Picts and Trolls united, too. It could pose a threat to the Land of the Fairies, she may think, though that, of course, is not true, either."

"So many lies," Almere cried. "What do I believe?"

The bird chirped and flew out the window, its task completed.

"There, it's going back to the fairy queen to report on how we disrespected her envoy."

"I don't really care," Almere said. "The fairies are lovely and sublime, and our dragons have an agreement with them, but I think we should keep our distance. We don't want foreign countries interfering in our politics."

"Why would she say that if it's not true?" asked Stannock, continuing to pace. He drew his huge double bladed shining war sword from its silver scabbard. "By the gods, I'm going to kill him."

"Stannock, we don't know if it's true." She whistled for her dragon, who appeared at the window almost instantly.

"Fire-Smasher," Almere began – and told him the bird's story.

He had failed his mistress. He hung his head. His father, Lockjaw, had told him last night to report this matter right away to the new king and queen, and Fire-Smasher had been afraid. He was afraid his suspicions were not correct. He doubted his own senses, being young and inexperienced. He hadn't wanted to make trouble for his dear companions in the Palace, and now he had made even more trouble by keeping still. He had failed his parents, too.

It is true, he began, and Almere blanched. Stannock's jaw clenched and a muscle twitched at the side of his jaw. *Or rather, I have suspicions. The Troll, Mindbender, and your brother are close like brothers themselves, and the Trolls and Picts are restless. They want more land, and I think Tevron has promised it to them.*

"You think?" Stannock plunged his sword into the side of a yellow silk wall. "You have to have more than feelings and suspicions, dragon."

It was Tevron who burnt the herbs of peace, that the Fairies gave Mindbender.

"Why would Mindbender go to the fairies? Is there an alliance there that we should be worried about?" Almere asked.

I don't think so. Fire-Smasher's wings beat rhythmically, outside the window, holding him up thirteen stories high.

"You don't *think* so," Stannock said and twisted his mouth so that he talked out of the side of his clenched jaw. His handsome face relaxed.

"I don't think there's anything to be worried about," he said to his wife and waved one hand to dismiss the red dragon. "This creature doesn't know anything for sure. For my own peace of mind, though, I'm going to take a couple of my captains to Peace River tomorrow and pay a little visit to Tevron and his good wife, and the Troll as well, while I'm there. I'm going to get to the bottom of this by myself. It's dangerous to pay much attention to idle gossip, but still, it needs to be checked out. I'll take my war drake, and Fire-Smasher can come along, as he's apparently worried. I want to see what he's worried about, or if this is a plot hatched by your dragon to discredit my family."

"Well, really," Almere said. "I'm going, too. And as for discrediting your family, there's not much more Fire-Smasher can do that we haven't done ourselves."

"Yes, my father sits in his quarters with his faithful manservant and plays with dolls and stares out the window for hours at a time. We did that."

"Your mother did that."

"There's peace in our kingdom for the first time in centuries and I'm going to make sure it stays that way. I didn't fight in the Troll Wars to come home and be pushed aside like a soft girl."

"I wonder about the Troll's constancy to the alliance," Almere said, "and why he would align himself with the fairies. The healers of Gracklen saved his life. He seemed most grateful and anxious to make a contract with the kingdom after being offered the lands to the northwest. That was what they wanted, or what they said they wanted. Now we're told it wasn't enough."

"Worrisome, dear." Stannock retrieved his sword from the wall and plunged it back into its scabbard.

"I think Mariette's had a calming influence on Tevron. I never told you, Stannock, but I didn't ever trust your half-brother, nor did I like him."

"Oh, I knew that. He followed you like a dog in heat."

"I don't think he'd hurt me. He did try to hurt *you*." They both remained silent, puzzling it out.

"Almere," Stannock continued, "we can't know anything sitting here like this. I'm getting my war drake saddled at first dawn, and my best captains with me, and I'll see what this is all about."

"I'm going, too," Almere said.

"What? No, you can't. Not in your condition, dear."

"What, now I'm not good enough to fight for my husband, fight for our kingdom, fight for our unborn child?"

"Of course, that's not what I meant."

"I think this is all for the best. Any feelings have to be sorted out, and any suspicions laid to bed."

"I agree with you there. I'll take my royal seal and make a pact with the Trolls and Picts right there in Tevron's house if I must. It's not safe for you and our child, though. I won't let you come."

"Who are you to tell me what I can do?" Almere objected. "However, I think your mother should be involved, too. At some other time. I'll let you go by yourself, with two handpicked captains. Devvid is faithful."

"Devvid was faithful to us, not to my father. The people don't trust him."

"Nonsense. I trust him with my life."

"Yes, and we may have to," Stannock said. "I'm leaving him to guard you while I'm gone."

"Take whom you will. I'll send Fire-Smasher with you. This all started with the Fairies, and my dragon, and they overheard something they may have misunderstood, but as I said, it's all for the best. I'm for getting it out in the open. I never did trust Tevron."

"So now you're saying the bird was right?"

Almere shifted in her chair. "I'm not saying that. I'm saying I don't know why the Fairies would align with Mindbender then send us the warning."

"Maybe Mindbender betrayed them."

"Suspicions, impressions, and hunches, that's all we have to go on. Let's get to bed early and you'll have an early start in the morning. I'll get Fire-Smasher prepared. He can carry the supplies and your court papers and writing materials; the royal seal should be carried on your person."

"Right." Stannock rubbed his chin. "I should spend more time in the settlements, anyhow."

"Ericaania ought to know," Almere said. "She hasn't been to Peace River since they moved down there."

"I don't think she likes Mariette."

"Tough toad," Almere said. "Tevron is her first-born son and she should acknowledge that."

"Sounds like you feel sorry for him."

Almere again shifted on her chair to a more comfortable position. She laced her fingers over her belly. "Maybe I do. I can see his point of view."

Stannock laughed. She stared at his thick erection and wondered if it was for her or for the situation. Her husband was born for battle. He was out of his element anywhere else. He needed a general over him and an army beneath him, a sword and spear and buckler in his hand – then he was complete. The black coral fertility stone glimmered on his bare, oiled chest. Her mouth was dry as he took her hand and led her to their bedroom.

Chapter Twenty-Eight

Ericaania was a black dot in a blue sky before Almere and Stannock realized she was gone to the settlements in the northwest. "She heard us talking last night and is upset," Almere explained, "and I understand why."

"She doesn't want her sons to be at odds." Stannock helped himself to another thimbleberry tart. Almere poured the coffee.

"Nor does she want her grandchildren endangered before they're even born," Almere said. "Tevron's a beast. He's nothing like his true father from what I understand. Malcoom was Ericaania's true love. She only married your father for political reasons."

"For expediency," he agreed. "But let's not talk about my father now. He's old, infirm, his heart is bad, and his mind gone. It's sad."

"Your mother poisoned him. The whole Palace knows that."

"She had no choice. He would have killed her first. Jon knows that, though he's faithful and loyal to Hakor. Still, I don't like to see the old man like this. And Jon is getting older, too, hardly able to care for his master anymore."

"I think it will sort itself out," Stannock said.

Almere sat with a thump opposite him at the table. "You always think it will sort itself out."

Stannock said nothing.

"We'll see for ourselves what's going on, out there in the badland. Solitude lends itself to intrigue and treachery. Tevron's alone out there, with his suspicious thoughts as always, Mariette who encourages them, and the ambitious Troll. The barrels of wine we send him down there don't help, either, I'm sure."

"Wine is good for the soul." Stannock finished the tart. He broke off a piece of soft bread to dip into a poached egg. "There's an old saying. Drown your troubles."

"I don't think Tevron is a drinker," Almere objected. "Unless he's changed."

"We don't know that. Still, he's my brother. We can't judge and condemn him on this flimsy evidence."

"We'll see what your mother says when she returns. Is she going to stay overnight?"

"I suppose it depends on the quality of the visit. Mariette is hospitable enough, and they have extra rooms."

Ericaania brushed a strand of grey hair from her eyes and faced Malcoom's son. He looked like his father but his habits were Hakor's. *No wonder*, she thought, *Hakor and I raised him. He never knew his father. He was four years old when Malcoom died in bed, his head severed from his body.*

She had married into a murdering family when she took a second husband. Now her son may be contemplating the abduction or murder of her grandchild. When would it stop? Forthright as always, Ericaania placed both hands on the wooden planks that made up their table and leaned toward her son. "Is it true?"

she asked. "Did Mindbender come over here with treasonous words? Do they want more land than they got, and does he want the Palace?"

Tevron considered the question, toying with his cup of dark burgundy wine. He gulped, upending the goblet in one swift motion, and poured another for her. "Where did you hear that, Mother?"

Mariette busied herself with the older children, reading from an old book, and the tutor pointed out nuances of thought and difficult words. Two young women played a game of "catch the can" outside with the younger children, who hooted and ran about. Lockjaw and Azazel grazed in the clearing beyond that. The fire burned out in the stove. Everything seemed quiet, peaceful even, thought Ericaania, before she answered her son.

"Almere's dragon had word, and the Fairies sent the Harpster bird to warn us." She decided to present the truth.

"The Fairies?" he snorted. "They have their wings in every pot, it seems. They also got to Mindbender, the big old Troll who can't mind his own business."

"Is it true?" she asked. "Are you making a deal with the Trolls for more land? And what does the Kingdom of Gracklen get in return? I thought you were here to negotiate for us, Tevron, not to line your own pockets."

She may have gone too far. Still, he was her son, and she knew him well.

"Yes, I'm discontented," he said. "Who wouldn't be? The Crown rightfully belongs to me, as the eldest son, and all my life I've lived outside the inner sanctum of the castle, made to feel like a second-rate prince, not even being sent to the front lines like my brother so I can show my courage in battle. I get a meager pension from the Palace; I don't live in the grand style of a proper prince. Yes, I think I got the short end of the tree when I was sent out here. And since my father died, I know I'm lucky to be allowed to live. That's followed me all my life, that my life is on eggshells and tenterhooks, as the ancients would have said. I studied, too, Mother. I have as good an education as Stannock, the hero in battle, but have never been allowed to prove myself or live the good life that a prince should enjoy. Even my wife is second-rate," he admitted, licking the wine from his lips.

"I'm sorry, Son," she said, sipping at the burgundy liquid. "I made a bargain with Hakor to spare our lives in return for my silence. Even so, the kingdom knows what was done. Your father was a mild man and ruled with a compassionate hand before Hakor came along. Yet he wasn't popular in the kingdom. Very few of his subjects tried to protest his death, which was presented as an accident at home. You'd think they would have tried to find out the truth."

"The truth?" snorted Tevron. "Not likely. Not with Hakor's iron hand on them. And a threat of the sword if anyone spoke out."

"That's true, and that was my concern, too, that he would take you away, give orders, and I would never see you again. I did my best. You've shown your softer side by caring for the children here, taking them in when it may have been our fault that their parents died by fire or the sword, and you are still a king's advisor. Be happy with that, my boy. Don't let your ambitions ruin the kingdom. It's always been my hope that my two sons would get along and perhaps rule together, but that was not to be. I have compassion for your plight, I really do, but there's nothing to be done besides perhaps talk to Stannock, and he has his father's stubbornness though he appears soft."

"His subjects say he's weak," Tevron scoffed. "Do you think so, Mother?"

"No," she said. "Of course not. He is a warrior and physically strong like Hakor, but not cunning and thoughtful like you or me. He doesn't rule with a steel arm like King Hakor did, and Hakor kept the kingdom together, after all."

"With a hundred-year war between the Trolls, Picts, and Gracklen."

"True enough." Ericaania toyed with her goblet. "We've put a stop to it, with Stannock's rule, and that in itself shows not only strength but wisdom. I'm aware that the plan came from you."

"Are you?" Tevron smiled and threw his cup onto the planked table. "That is true, Mother, it was my idea. I shared it with Almere the night before Stannock came home from the Troll Wars. Now I'm in charge of the settlement and negotiations, and my wisdom is being questioned."

"I suppose that's true," Ericaania said, "but we mustn't give away more land, nor must we endanger the Crown." She was getting close to her own suspicions, the ideas that the Fairy's bird and Almere's dragon had planted the night the moons were full.

"I won't." Tevron lied, and he knew his mother knew it. What could he do? He couldn't admit to treasonous thoughts. His groin stirred within his tight black pants when he looked over at Mariette. She was always a plump and comforting woman in bed. He could have done worse. But Stannock – Stannock had Almere. Tevron grimaced, feeling sorry for himself.

"No one understands you," Ericaania admitted. "Least of all I. But I know you better than most, perhaps, and I want to help you. I'll do something about your low status, Son, if it's the last thing I do."

"That will help." Tevron tore the leather cords from the top of the crimson shirt he wore. He missed the swastika cross he had worn since a child. It was far across the Agave Sea now, making trouble for the Fairy Queen. Unless it was true that Fairies were immune to curses. Damn.

Across the room, Mariette finished the lesson and closed her books with a snap. The tutor began to chat in a low voice with a couple of the children who asked questions. He opened a thick book and stabbed his finger at the text. The younger children outside whooped and rushed in the door like a flight of excited young dragons.

"Time for your snacks." Mariette thumped her way across the wooden floor to the kitchen. She took out the cut fruit and cheese, poured the dragon's milk, and set it all in front of the children with some help from the young women who had herded the children into the building.

"I think I'll pay a visit to the Troll." Ericaania moved surreptitiously toward the door. "It's been a nice visit."

"What, you're leaving already?" Mariette raised her eyebrows. "You've hardly stayed at all."

"I know. I can't. I have to get back," Ericaania apologized. "I wanted to talk to my son."

"Oh, I see. Court business. All right, then. Far be it from me to interrupt."

The Queen Mother leaned forward. "I think you can help, Mariette. I'm enlisting your aid, too. We must make things easier for Tevron in the kingdom. He has a great responsibility here, and I fear he's not getting the guidance nor support a king's son needs and should have. After all, he was raised in the Palace, in a sheltered environment. As well, things are different now that my husband is indisposed."

"Yeah, they sure are." Mariette put a large iron kettle onto the fire. "I don't think it's a good idea for you to see Mindbender, though, Mother. I just don't see that it can stir up anything but trouble."

"Yes," Tevron agreed with a scowl. "The big old Troll is trouble."

"My coven and I healed him when he was sorely wounded," the Queen Mother reminded them. "Surely he doesn't forget that. He doesn't owe us anything, but isn't there such a thing as gratitude in the world of the Trolls?"

"I don't think so, frankly," Mariette said, sitting down next to her mother-in-law. "I'm making tea. Stay for some?"

"Yes," Ericaania said, "tea would be nice. I especially like your thimbleberry tea with honey, dear."

"Oh, you've had that before, have you? Well, coming right up, Your Majesty," Mariette joked.

"My dragon is feeding with yours. I must go to him and see that he's all right. Dragons are not patient creatures."

Mariette smiled. "Tevron's beast, Azazel, is a fiery mount if any there were, always straining at his reins, eager to take the saddle off, and eager to soar into our sky to meet with his pals from across Gracklen. They come here often, the dragons do; they do get around, and without their riders, too."

"We're aware of that, and of course, they have their own court and their own families and lives. We humans are lucky to have such loyal companions, in my view, and if some are a bit wild, like Azazel, well, that is their original nature."

"He doesn't like me," Tevron said.

Sure enough, the two dragons were speaking of that in the clearing, Fire-Smasher of course, being more loyal than most, listening more than speaking his mind.

I AM THE BATTLE, Azazel roared. *I AM FATE.* The clearing blazed with fire. Some small shrubs burned in a row along the base of the Thurtle tree.

"Your energies are wasted here," Fire-Smasher agreed. "But he is the King's son. That's an honor."

"Honor? I fought in the Troll Wars and defeated huge armies. The King's major general himself has ridden on my back. Now look at me. Stuck here in the outback by order of King Stannock. Life was far better under the old king. We had honor then."

"We have honor now," Fire-Smasher said. "A change is sweeping across Gracklen. A change is coming to Draxxt itself. The lands across the seas call for the Trolls to repopulate them, and I think Tevron is going to see that."

"The Trolls want more and more. They want our land. The nasty king's sons are going to give it to them. The battles will never stop until the

Trolls are in the Palace. That is the day the dragons will fly back to the lands from which we
came, long ago, before the humans enslaved us."

"I don't feel enslaved." Fire-Smasher spit on
the burning bushes and the fire sizzled out to
ash.

"You are young. You don't remember the old
times."

"They were never as good as you recall. That's
what my Almere says."

"Hum. You've become the favorite of the royal
family. I can see where your loyalties lie."

"All dragons are loyal to their riders. It was
the oath we took thousands of years ago."

The fighting dragon snorted white smoke and
flames. "You said yourself that change is coming
to Draxxt. That could be a good thing."

"It could," Fire-Smasher said. "We agree.
What it will be, I don't know, but I sort of think
we're in post-apocalyptic times, good friend."

"They've talked of the Old Religion?"

"Yes. It's legal now."

"Nobody understands that holy book. Maybe
the healers do, the witches and warlocks. Or the

ancient order of monks, that still exist in the Land of the Fairies, protected by them."

Just then, Ericaania glided into the clearing. "Time to go, darling."

"Where's Lockjaw?" snorted Azazel.

"He's giving his son a chance to try out different riders," Ericaania explained. "It's part of Fire-Smasher's education."

"I think Big Red's too attached to his companion, Queen Almere. Always has been. I've seen them together. An unnatural little human, she is, with that wild black hair, her brown face and blue eyes. There's something fairylike about her, and I don't trust the Fairies."

Ericaania considered the comment.

"You might be right." She led Fire-Smasher to the edge of the glen, where his golden saddle and reins of fire awaited them. Certainly, she knew that Almere's mother went back to the Land of the Fairies after her father was killed. Did the Fairy Queen hide her still? Did she know the truth about Almere's mother? No one knew why the girl had been left abandoned, with a dowry for a princess, and a promise to wed Stannock when they were of age. Ericaania had long ago taken the place of a mother to the girl.

Wouldn't it be amazing if Almere's mother lived? Ericaania would go home today, she would leave the great Troll where he was, and she would do something about her eldest son's misery if she died trying. For Tevron was as precious to her in his own way as was Stannock, the golden-haired boy who never did a thing wrong. Almere's mother chose to abandon the girl, and Ericaania, for her part, wished to let it remain that way.

She boarded Fire-Smasher and began the long trek home. They were a streamer of smoke and flame in the face of the two remaining suns, heading back to the Palace, where Almere and Stannock debated the name of the child. If it were a girl they would call her Ericaania Joy, and if it were a boy they would call him Stannock the Second.

"I prefer Hakor the Second," Stannock objected. "But you're always right, dear."

Of course, they were both wrong. The birthing would see to that.

"She didn't hear," Tevron said, and patted Mariette's ample butt.

"Didn't hear what, husband?" she asked, fussing with the plates and knives.

"Nothing," Tevron said and laughed. "You'll hear about it soon enough."

"I'll hear about it now or never," she said. "I don't like being kept in the dark."

Tevron laughed again. "You didn't seem to mind last night." She hit him hard on the shoulder.

"Sassy." They went to bed; the children having been settled for the night.

Chapter Twenty-Nine

"Fine, you convinced me." Stannock held his wife's waist as the red dragon bucked and gyred beneath them. "What if the baby's born in midair?" He glanced far down at the undulating landscape below, all green, lush, flower-strewn, and ice-capped mountains coming up in the distance. Almere laughed like a Fairy, all tinkling bells and delight.

"I'm looking forward to a nice cup of tea at Tevron's place, with Mariette, and we haven't properly thanked her for the beautiful coverlet she sewed."

"Let's not forget she's a maid." Stannock sniffed. Fire-Smasher spun smoke rings in the air before them. Wind shrieked past their ears and blew Almere's black hair into a devil halo about her face. Stannock laughed, too, his wife's powerful arms guiding the dragon.

"She's good for Tevron. He needs a strong hand."

"Me, too." Stannock tightened his grip on his wife's belly. He slid his hand up to cup her breast. "How's that for a hand?" She pulled his fingers off her bodice, still laughing.

"It's a beautiful day for a ride. I wish Ericaania could have come with us."

"She chose to visit yesterday. I know she loves my brother, too. He's difficult to love. I think she feels guilty about his place in the kingdom."

"He doesn't let anyone forget about it."

They swooped and soared until the marshy areas of the badlands appeared. They could see the sprawling settlements of the Trolls and Picts in Many Waters, and not too far from that, the building that was the orphanage. Fire-Smasher prepared his mighty thighs for a landing in the clearing near Tevron's home. A magnificent drake pranced in the glen, clearly expecting them. They landed near a huge Thurtle tree and Fire-Smasher's riders slid off his mighty back. Stannock alighted first, held out his arms for his wife to join him, but she pealed with laughter and skipped beside him, evading his reach. "I don't need help," she explained. "But thank you just the same."

"You're endangering our child," Stannock objected. "Be more careful. This isn't a joy ride a year ago when you were slimmer and healthier."

"Nonsense," she said. "I've never been so healthy. My doctor says I can do whatever I want, and that exercise is good for me."

"I'm glad he's so modern," Stannock said. "You and my mother worry the heck out of me."

Tevron strode into the glen. "Welcome, brother." He threw a smoldering glance at Almere. "You're looking good, Almere. Ready to give us an heir? I found out about it just last night. Thanks to you both for letting me know."

"Sorry, Tev," Stannock apologized. "She just started to show. Didn't say anything in case something happened, you know. Being cautious."

"So, you're not barren after all." Tevron chewed on a fingernail.

Behind him, Mariette threw her arms open in greeting. "Welcome, sister-in-law. We heard the good news."

Stannock threw the reins to the ground. Fire-Smasher brushed against Azazel and made mind contact.

So, it's true, Azazel thought. *The King's wife will have a child. So many babies in our clan, too. It must be something in the air, like that odd smell that my companion burned a few sun cycles ago, that with Daemon's rising permeated our world, to the Land of the Fairies and back.*

I heard about that. Fire-Smasher snorted and set fire to a shrub at the other end of the clearing. *Oops.*

Azazel puffed himself up, so he appeared even larger. *My own master is not weak like yours.*

Fire-Smasher huffed and great clouds of smoke billowed into the air above their heads. Scales fell like silver tears.

The humans paced the short distance to the house. Children milled in the yard, played with colored balls and shouted to their friends. Mariette rounded them up with outstretched arms.

"Now, children, we have guests. Go play in the back."

"Hello," Almere greeted and smiled to the children. A small child gazed up at her with hooded eyes, hair black and curling around his shoulders.

"Why is your dragon crying?" Timothie asked.

"He isn't," Almere said, and her eyebrows lifted. Her mouth formed an "O." "We've had a long ride and he's tired."

"Do his scales fall off when he's tired?" asked a small girl. She twisted her red polka dot dress through her fingers. Before Almere could answer, the two children joined their friends, who hooted and shouted around the building to the back. She could hear them playing "Anti high over" with a ball on the rooftop.

"Stannock." Almere put a hand on her husband's strong arm. "Is Fire-Smasher sad?"

He glanced back at the glen where the two dragons rubbed necks. "No." He shook his head. "He's just tired. He was quite excited to get here and meet his friend again. They have a lot to talk about because Tevron's dragon doesn't see a lot of the others now that he's here in the outback. He must feel banished, after the excitement of the Troll Wars where he was a hero."

My companion, the King, is not weak. Fire-Smasher munched on a small rodent that had chanced unluckily across his path. *He's sensitive and tired from the wars.*

A warrior is not tired from battle.

He was hurt. He's still gaining strength. His brother didn't join the battle. He's the human, if any, who's weak. Tevron the Timid. Stannock the Just.

Stop rhyming. It's not funny. Azazel stretched his long neck toward the sky. *I'm not happy with my rider. And he plots against the kingdom. I've a mind to tell the King while he's here.*

He knows.

How does he know? Did you tell him?

Fire-Smasher shrugged. Scales littered the grass. *Yes. But they don't believe me.*

He's not only weak, he's stupid.

A dragon shouldn't think so of humans. It's not right.

Why not? Azazel's thoughts were stern. *Because they came to Draxxt thousands of years*

289

ago, on a metal dragon belching fire, with science and magic we didn't understand, back there in the dawn of our history? Because they tamed us? I have an urge to turn my head and eat my black prince.

Fire-Smasher gasped. *No!*

Yes. Like days of old, when dragons fought with the humans and lost.

That's against every precept of our clans. We're here to protect and serve.

Azazel preened and hovered in the air for a brief moment on a pillar of fire and smoke. *We're slaves, Fire-Smasher. Even our names are given to us by our humans.*

They protect and care for us, too. I would miss my home in the castle. What would we do? It would be like the old, wild days of our ancestors when we foraged and fought monsters in the woodlands and mountains. When brave humans came against us and subdued us. No, I won't go back.

Do you know my name is a fierce fighting name, and we live up to the names we're given. Names have a spiritual significance. Mine is a great warrior's name, from the Book of Abraham, a very old magic book in the human's history. See, even that is not our dragon lore. It's something weak and from our riders. I wish we had been left alone, free to—

Fire-Smasher had never heard such treacherous speech from a dragon. *To what? To kill, maim, and die? You are surely the mount for the King's brother. He's just the same as you.*

I've thought of that. We may be well matched, except he's no warrior.

No, he's treacherous and cunning. But that is not a weak man. That's a clever man. They have a myth, from very ancient times, about a man called Odysseus, who was cunning and treacherous, not a great warrior at all, yet a whole epic was written about him by a blind poet of the time.

I don't care. Azazel shrugged and went back to grazing. Fire-Smasher curled up in the shade of the large Thurtle, which drooped with pink blossoms at this time of year, approaching Draxxt's spring.

In Tevron's house, Mariette served huge bowls of stew and hot fresh bread from the oven. Her husband's family ate and then pushed back their plates.

"Very good meal," Stannock said. He scratched his rounded biceps. "You've married well, brother."

Tevron glowered. *He wanted to marry me,* Almere thought.

"If it wasn't for the charm, she would never have caught me," Tevron pointed out.

"That's right, husband." Mariette simpered. "I was the lucky one."

Tevron patted her plump hand. "I was the lucky one." He stared at Stannock with envy for his brother's wife. Stannock stared back.

"What's this I hear about Mindbender?" Stannock changed the subject. It was time they got to the point. "I hear he's been over here, spouting mutiny."

"No, not mutiny," Tevron said. Mariette began to clean up the plates and Tevron took a dry towel and helped her. Stannock and Almere sat and watched.

"What then? He wants more land? For the Trolls and Picts, or just for the Trolls? The Picts have been quiet."

"That's worrisome," Tevron said. "When the Picts are quiet."

"They leave their politics up to the Trolls. But they're good fighters," Stannock said.

"Not like me?

Mariette rattled the dishes, prompting Tevron to put away bowls and cutlery. Mariette wiped out the basins, swept the floor, and they both sat down with their guests.

"You had your place in the Palace with the old king. I enjoy battle. You don't. We all have our place."

"Oh, I enjoy a good fight." Tevron smirked and smacked his fist on the long wooden trestle table at which they sat. Mariette went to feed the children in the next room. Their chatter and laughter drowned out the conversation among the adults.

"As for Mindbender and the Trolls," his brother continued. "Yes, he's been here. We've discussed a fairer settlement for them. More land, and perhaps..."

"Perhaps the Palace?" Stannock asked. He put his hand on his sword hilt, his swinging silver dagger perilously close to his hand.

"The remnants of peace remain in the land. The burning herbs were a mistake, but they wafted all over Gracklen and the lands beyond."

"They lulled us into thinking war isn't inevitable."

"You were ever warlike, brother. Like the Lord Hakor, your father."

"And you are more like Hakor than I ever was," countered Stannock. Escaping the mounting tension, Almere joined Mariette with the children, ladling their stew into huge steaming bowls, buttering the bread, and cutting up fruit and cream for their dessert. The two men faced one another.

"This is a warning." Stannock flexed his muscular torso. He wiped food off his blond beard and ran a free hand through the mop of fair hair, much like Hakor's had been before it turned grey.

"A warning from you? What are you going to do, bring me back to the Palace? I know you don't want that."

"No, although you would be welcome there. You and Mariette have done a good thing here, helping with the settlers, serving as go-between amongst the various tribes, picking up with the orphans where their parents left off, trying to locate the parents – no, you're needed here. But not for intrigue. Not for treason."

"Treason? That's a strong word, brother." Tevron put his hand on his own sword, a sturdy steel blade that swung in a leathern scabbard from his hip.

"What of our child? It's been suggested you have designs on her life."

"Her? What happened to a king?" Tevron sneered.

"We don't know if the child is a princess or prince. My mother is rather fond of saying the child is a girl, destined to lead our kingdom to many years of peace and comfort."

"She is a healer; she can see into the future, but not that far," Tevron growled. "The child is an abomination. I am the rightful ruler of Draxxt."

"Then what I have been told is correct." Stannock stood for a moment in thought, his head bowed, his forehead furrowed. "You have plans for the Crown."

"Of course. What do you think? Wouldn't you? I've been denied my rightful place, as eldest son."

"You're the son of Malcoom, not the rightful heir."

"I can command an army behind me, brother, that will defeat you. You should have died on the battleground."

"We'll fight for the right!" Stannock shouted and drew his sword.

GILGAMESH! cried the Fire-Smasher from the glen, and Azazel smirked.

Chapter Thirty

The brothers fought through the yard, the glen, and the hills, all day and well into the evening. The sky turned grey and a wind picked up the dust as they battled, with spits of rain falling toward the afternoon. Tevron took the first blow on his left forearm, drawing scarlet drops of blood that spurted onto his tunic and stained his leather bodkin. He tore off the tunic and bodkin, bare to the waist, snarled at Stannock, and lunged. His sword hacked air. Stannock parried and danced forward, slashing expertly, while his brother placed both hands on the hilt of his steel weapon and roared a challenge. Sweat poured from their faces and backs. The clang and jar of their battle could be heard across the length of the settlements, where all wise citizens stayed indoors.

Mariette herded the children into the building and the helpers made up a strapping big meal of cheese, bread, grains, meat, and a marvelous sauce concocted by boiling down vegetables from their garden, with herbs and spices from the same garden, all served from the huge iron pot that swung over the flames. Almere sang to them, songs of old of fighting men and women and explained about the legends that spurred boys and girls to become warriors.

Stannock leaned into the battle with his entire weight as he leveled another blow at the stocky but shorter man. Tevron was bleeding but his strong legs propelled him sideways to evade the charge.

I'm hurt, he thought. *Almere is watching, my true love. Stannock has the Crown, he has her, and everything I always wanted. I can't let him touch me now.*

With both hands, he brought down his steel blade on Stannock's sword, knocking it out of the way, then quickly recovered and slashed at his brother's inner thigh to bring him to the ground, but Stannock dodged. Tevron advanced, slashing wildly, but Stannock was grim and backed into the clearing where the dragons watched, his back against the red dragon as he parried.

He's a madman, Stannock thought. *I didn't know my brother was capable of such strength.*

Tevron tore through the shrubs, slashing at branches, and lunged at his brother, who backed to one side near his dragon. Stannock sprang and advanced, also slashed but more expertly and with purpose. He was the more experienced swordsman, but his brother had practiced in the same fields as he when a boy and possessed more strength.

Fire-Smasher roared and raised his mighty head, flames billowed from his jaws, and the other fierce fighting dragon, Azazel, laughed and quoted the Gilgamesh saga as much as he could remember, as dragons do, for they love a good epic poem. *There, my dark prince is proving himself to be more of a warrior than we thought.*

"We'll take to the skies," shouted Tevron and mounted Azazel, who shouted with laughter and snorted fire and smoke, spiraled up into the spitting rain, and was followed closely by Fire-Smasher, who bore the new king on his back, each dragon not saddled but controlled with reins of fire.

Kill him! roared Azazel, almost drunk with the ecstasy of battle, and Fire-Smasher soared into the eye of the storm with Stannock on his back.

A north wind howled and rain slashed sideways at their bodies as the men fought from the backs of their mounts, gyred closer and brushed the sides of the huge beasts. The brothers leaned into the fight as their dragons soared past one another, turned and danced in the now driving rain. The dragons lunged with huge jaws at one another, while the brothers bled and struck again and again.

Below, the villagers watched. Mariette and Almere tended to the children inside, blanching with every blow they heard from above.

"They're crazy," Almere said.

"They've been at each other's throats as long as I've known them," Mariette commented, brushing crumbs off a table. "Good for them. I hope they kill each other."

"Men," Almere said. "I hope Fire-Smasher isn't injured."

Mariette laughed. "Not to mention our husbands."

"Do you think they'll be finished by nightfall?"

"You can always stay here, sister." Mariette sat with a plunk on a soft cushion and cuddled two or three small children into her plump embrace. "Now, now," she cooed. "Isn't this cozy?"

"Why are they fighting?" asked a child.

"Because they have to," Almere explained. "They're brothers, and they love each other, but they don't know it."

"So why are they up there in the air making each other bleed?"

"Because they are men."

"Oh."

"Will I be like that when I grow up?" Timothie Hill asked.

"Probably," Mariette said, and her mouth twisted. "Let's all have a story now, shall we?" She told them a story of when their world was new and the men and women arrived on a great metal dragon, with fire and smoke, and the real dragons befriended them after a big fight, because that's what humans and dragons do.

"I understand," said the small boy.

"Do you?" Almere began to sing again. She sang an old ballad of war and peace, and the children didn't listen at all but began to play amongst themselves with their ball, indoors, which they weren't allowed to do, but today was different.

In the pelting rain, high above the badland, the two brothers fought until at last the dragons tired and descended. Tevron and Stannock slid from their mounts and shook hands.

"You're right," Stannock said. "You should have been king as well. Let's call a halt to this madness, brother."

"Together? Never," Tevron felt too weary to lift his sword, but the bleeding had stopped, and he felt a wave of exaltation wash through him. *Vindicated.*

"Oh, you want to continue to fight?" Stannock's sword lay in the mud, but he struggled to pick it up. Both men collapsed into the mud, their hands around the other's neck.

The Trolls watched, too – they had stridden near, and peered with their huge elongated eyes at the spectacle of their new king and his advisor having at it in the clouds and now the mud. *What will this mean to us?* they asked the mighty Troll, their leader Mindbender, who refused to budge from his hut at the edge of Many Waters. He shrugged. *What else? The humans are crazy, and it means we won't get the Palace or more lands, I suspect. We'll have to fight.*

The settlers, too, asked themselves what the outcome would be of such an epic battle. Mariette and Almere left the children with their helpers and their lessons and play, and marched into the clearing to collect their husbands.

The two men lay in the mud, their swords clutched in their hands, and the glen rang with their hearty laughter as they rolled and clutched each other.

"Laughing, are you?" asked Mariette.

Almere led Fire-Smasher to a sheltering Thurtle tree at the edge of the clearing. She took a cloth and wiped him clean, murmuring to her dragon as she did, "Good boy, Fire-Smasher, what an awful thing to have to do."

Azazel nudged Tevron, who reached out with a muddy hand and patted the fierce beast on his scaly head. "You all right, boy?"

Of course. We were born for this.

Fire-Smasher purred and struck a pose with his chest puffed out. *We're a warrior.* Fire dribbled from his nostrils. *I think we're even bleeding.*

"No, you're not." Almere wiped him down with a thick towel.

The two brothers picked themselves up from the mud, bleeding and filthy, and confronted Mariette, who stood with hands on her hips and frowned.

"I'm starving for some of that good stew," Tevron said casually, as though the fight had been nothing more than play, and they staggered toward the house with arms around one another's shoulders.

Chapter Thirty-One

Mindbender's receiving hall was filled with Trolls and Picts as they met to discuss their concerns. Their plan to have more land may be endangered because of the apparent truce between their Palace Administrator and the King.

"As well," one young Troll stated, "We want the Palace."

"That doesn't seem forthcoming," Mindbender said. "Realistically. It was an agreement between the Administrator and myself, and now it looks as though the peace in our land may be on their heads and still in their hands."

"After all," another young Troll spoke up, "they won the war."

"No, it was a truce," insisted a blue-stained Pict, throwing his spear at the far wall. "We were betrayed by our leaders. We could have kept on fighting and won." They all turned and glared at Mindbender, the engineer of the truce.

"You forget," he said, "the massive deaths and injuries we suffered at their hands when the Queen invaded with her dragons. That was followed up by the rest of their armies, which effectively put us out of commission. All we had to fight with were hand weapons. They came from the skies, and then their fresh forces overcame us. You forget, young Spellbinder."

"You told us we'd have more land, the fertile land to the south and east," another Pict objected. "We've been ruled by the Trolls for too long. Our forces are just as effective as yours, but you don't pay us any mind at the negotiating tables, Mindbender."

A general murmur of agreement swept throughout the room. Mindbender wiped his greasy mouth with one hand as he picked up an enormous goblet of ale with the other. The Picts were on one side of the room and the Trolls on the other, pushing and arguing amongst themselves. *If I don't gain control, I'll have lost my leadership.* Mindbender stood to his full height and roared. "Silence!"

The room grew still. A bird perched on the window ledge and sang a pretty song, but it wasn't the Harpster bird, and Mindbender welcomed the diversion. He swept one arm to indicate the little animal.

"Like this bird, who isn't spying on us like some do, and you know who I mean..."

The hall erupted in angry shouts. "Silence!" he roared once more and stood on the broad planked table. His head brushed the rafters in the immense room. "You all know I've been speaking to the Fairies, who have vowed to help us. Their Harpster bird reports to the Fairy Queen on all activities in Gracklen, and they haven't forgotten our land across the sea, either, where we came from before we took Many Waters from the human kingdom. We can go back..."

"No!" His words were greeted by a chorus of pushing and jostling creatures, angry fists raised.

"You all know the new king has declared freedom of religion and education in Gracklen. I have spoken with Merrywether, the Fairy Queen. We met in her crystal palace where there are many marvels, including a tall library of forbidden books. She loaned me some of the old books so that we may know the truth. For those who can read the strange human tongue, they tell of events long ago which we knew only from myth."

He continued, "At first I didn't believe her. It might make a difference to how we view the humans, whom we thought invaded Draxxt thousands of years ago and subdued the dragons, Trolls, and Picts. To our everlasting shame and disadvantage. That is our myth."

"Yes, it's true! Yes, down with the humans!"

"The myth of the metal dragon they came in seems correct, but it wasn't a dragon. They came from another planet, with only one star…"

"Impossible! How would they light the sky with only one sun? How would they heat their world?"

"Their sun was far larger than ours, and they had a shorter night and day. But they did come in a metal ship…"

"It wasn't a ship! How would a ship fly?"

"This ship flew through space, it was made of metal, and it had an engine which belched fire. That's what the old books say, and it makes more sense than a metal dragon, to me."

"Here," Mindbender continued. "I've been studying these texts." He held up a couple of ancient books in his hand. "See for yourself. It's our history. The Fairy Queen was right. We seem to be of the same stock as humans. We came to Draxxt with them."

"No, we didn't. We've always lived on Draxxt, with the Fairies and the dragons. That's a lie!"

"The humans gave birth to the Picts, who were a smaller mutation, and they eventually began to color themselves to differentiate from their human parents. Trolls – well, we were the result of genetic experiments."

"No, we weren't! There's no such thing."

"Yes, the humans were very scientific back then; they didn't use magic as they do now. Everything was different. The experiments produced what they called monsters and they began to call us 'Trolls' and 'Picts.' There was a civil war and we aligned ourselves against the humans, and the dragons took the side of the humans, who won the war back then as well as now."

"No, they didn't! That's a lie." The hall seemed out of control. Mindbender used the powers of his mind to subdue the lesser Trolls and Picts.

"The dragons have served humans ever since," he said. "I myself am hundreds of years old, and as I'm so much different and larger than the rest of you, I must have been the result of an experiment, too. I don't like it. But it's right here in the books, and in our lore, and the Fairy Queen agrees with me. The Fairies have been on this planet they call Minth since time immemorial. They're very old and very wise…"

"No, they're not! They're a pawn for the humans, like you are, traitor!"

Mindbender struggled to regain control of the room. "The Fairies didn't get involved in the original wars, but stepped in later and stripped the humans of their science. With magic. Ever since then, there's been this rift between the humans and the Trolls and Picts, and the Fairies have kept their distance, other than making sure that nobody destroys the planet. As they think we're about to do."

"The Fairies are traitors, too. Magic is superior to science."

"I agree," Mindbender said. "Their science almost destroyed Draxxt. Magic is superior and just as powerful, but in a better way. I also think that we are superior to the humans, being the result of science and not creation."

"Yes, we are superior! But we never were human. You are lying to us, Mindbender. Burn the books!"

Mindbender's gnarled green face turned a different shade of chartreuse, and he blew fire from his mouth like a dragon. The bird left the ledge. After a little more heated discussion, the Trolls and Picts left the room, vowing to have revenge on the humans and, probably, Mindbender himself as their emissary. The last Troll turned and shook his fist at his leader, who was well into his cups by then. Another bird with a purple chest listened outside, unseen.

Mindbender looked out on a beautiful, cloudless day. He had one more journey to take.

Chapter Thirty-Two

The remnants of peace remained in the land but the Trolls' toxic murmurings were more powerful. "Get the Fairies on our side," they urged their leader, Mindbender, and he nodded his massive head in agreement.

Shaking his hairy fist, an old painted Pict stood on a table and squealed, "We'll never have peace until the humans are gone. Your friend, the dark prince, doled out marshy land to us like it was his own to portion, and he is a frugal and cheap man, works for the new king, and is no friend to the Trolls and Picts."

"The Pict is right. He never meant to be friends with us," roared a young Troll. "You were taken in by the promise of personal land and riches."

"Silence!" Mindbender strode to the back of the room and picked up the offending Picts and the young Troll by their necks. He shook them so violently that their teeth chattered and their arms swung out, knocking a flagon of ale from the table. "You forget who you're talking to, vermin! Our armies were in disarray and our young men and women dead or dying when I saw the old queen and her dragons fly back to the Palace successful, and Major General Stannock at the head of a battalion of half-dead men. Their dragons won the war for them. Tevron, the dark prince, seemed generous at first. It was his idea to give us the land to the northwest of the Agave Sea, which we called Many Waters, and we've moved into the tributaries as well, pushing the humans further southeast. We needed diplomats, not warriors, at that time."

"But that time has passed," squeaked the Pict dangling from Mindbender's great hand. "We need warriors, and we need the dragons on our side."

"That will never happen." Mindbender released the trio and they fell in a heap on the dirt floor. "The dragons are bound to the humans from long ago. They've sworn a contract, and a dragon never goes back on its word."

"The Fairies, then." The room became silent as the Trolls and Picts thought it over. "Yes, the Fairy Queen has magic and shares our dislike of the humans. Let's visit the Fairies again, get them on our side, and use their magic to overthrow the Kingdom of Gracklen, which could have been ours."

A thoughtful old Troll interjected. "What's in it for the Fairies? They'll want to know."

"Why, our old ways back, and the humans don't have to be killed. They can be banished to the far reaches of our old lands across the sea, where we came from, where we were kept for centuries until our leaders freed us."

"Don't forget who that leader was." Mindbender puffed out his mottled chest. "We've made inroads. Don't forget it."

Tevron and Mariette left the children in the care of their capable helpers and flew to the Palace, fearing for their lives, as the badlands were no longer safe with talk of Troll invasion at any time. No one had seen Mindbender for a few days and it was feared he had gone off to recruit help for a takeover of Peace River and even beyond. All types of gossip swirled in the settlements, and many settlers had packed up their belongings and gone south to lands just as fertile but at a distance from the impending trouble.

"But the children," Mariette worried on the flight home. Azazel, the fierce beast, bucked and snorted in anticipation of a future fight with the Trolls they had left behind. "They should be relocated, too. They're much too close to the troubles."

Handling the fiery reins with an expert hand, her husband glowered at the landscape beneath. She clung to the back of the saddle. Her gown billowed in the wind created by Azazel's plunging. "The Trolls are nothing but trouble," he agreed. "The Picts are little nuisances with arrows of fire that prick and destroy. I'll talk to my brother when we return of bringing the children to the Palace. They could easily be transported on a fleet of our Palace dragons led by Faerydust and the two other dragonesses, who are more gentle than the drakes like this mount here." He flicked the reins and Azazel leaped high into the blue burning sky. From below, villagers sheltered their eyes with their hands and wondered, as they talked about yet another black flying dot in the face of the triple suns.

Stannock welcomed his brother and Mariette as they circled the castle ramparts and the guards let down the mighty gates. He stood in the outer courtyard and Mariette hugged him. Legs planted on firm ground again, Tevron swaggered to the wall and looked over. The valley below and the blue mountains in the distance seemed tranquil. He frowned.

"There's talk of relocating the Trolls and Picts back to their old homeland across the Agave Sea, where the buildings and castles are in disrepair but may still be habitable," Stannock explained to the couple later, over cups of wine and plates of fine meat, grapes, and cheese. "Spies have been ordered across the land to report back to us of any suspicious movements."

Hands clasped on her enormous belly, Almere joined them. "Another long war appears to be imminent. I fear for the child."

"When do you think he will be born?" Mariette asked. "It's a hard time for a child, I agree."

"Soon, I hope." Almere adjusted her pale blue gown and smiled the way only a new mother can. "The Queen Mother is very pleased, though. Nothing can take away our joy."

Mariette smiled in return. "Tevron and me have talked about bringing the orphans here to the castle, for safekeeping. What do you think about that, Stannock?"

"It's a good idea. We have to be cautious, especially where our people are concerned there in the settlements. I've ordered an evacuation. My good Captain Devvid is to be in charge. He's taken a second wife now, a fierce fighting woman from the army ranks, and together they've been dispatched with a corps to oversee the move."

"Could we get the children brought out at the same time as the settlers move? Or will they be going with the people there to the southeast?"

Stannock considered. "I think they'll be safer here in the Palace, though in these troubled times, no one is safe from Mindbender and his thugs."

Tevron glared at Almere. "We haven't heard of the old Troll in several days. I wonder what he's up to?"

Stannock pushed his plate back and got up to pace the floor. "The Fairy Queen, known as Merrywether, and the troll Mindbender have already met, to what end I don't know, but that started the peace herbs that have misted the sky since then. A Troll has magic, too, but nothing can touch the Fairies."

"I thought the Trolls and the Fairies were in on this thick. Merrywether has never liked us," Tevron said.

"She wouldn't stoop to compromise a possible peace on Gracklen. I don't believe that," Almere said. "She tricked you to burn the herbs, after all, hoping to settle some magic on the countryside that would divert talk of war and bring our people to a mellower state of mind."

"We'll see." Tevron's words were directed at Stannock. He barely looked at his sister-in-law. Mariette put a plump hand on her husband's arm.

"What is it between you and our sister, Tev?" she asked. "Look at her, acknowledge the child, put bygones behind us."

Tevron shifted in his seat, the wounds from his swordplay with Stannock still evident, but minor. He put out a hand like a piece of meat. "You're right," he said. "I have what I want. Mariette and I have no child to take our place. Let's settle the orphans in and welcome the new prince."

"You can be known as king in my place, when I'm away, and live here as co-ruler," Stannock offered. "You may be crowned next Freisday, brother, and we will together be invincible. Sound like a good plan?"

"I don't have the Palace skills necessary nor the training in arms that you have, Stann," Tevron said. "Though I can whip your arse, can't I?" He chuckled.

Stannock grinned and struck his brother on his sore shoulder. Tevron winced and smiled. "The two brothers as king. Sounds good. Yet behind us is there this sadness, the old king in his dotage, playing with dolls in the basement of the Palace."

"I know." Almere heaved to her feet. "I visit him sometimes, and Ericaania often. He doesn't recognize us. It's sad. Jon is his only lifeline to the rest of us, and to the life he once led."

"Yet he tried to murder our mother." Tevron pushed away his plate as well and got to his feet. His muddy boots tracked on the clean tiled floor.

"Tev," Mariette protested, "we look like farmers, here in this clean Palace."

"Do you remember when you worked there, above the Queen's quarters?" her husband asked. "It seems like a millennium ago."

"It does seem at least centuries ago," Mariette said. "I'm grateful I'm out of there."

Tevron moved to her side and patted her hand. "Yet you bettered yourself, for your husband."

Mariette blushed. "I'd rather not talk of it.".

"I don't blame you." Almere trundled to Mariette's side and hugged her. The baby moved within her womb. "Here, Esmeralda and Judith," Almere said to her maids who hovered nearby. "Please show the new king and his wife to their rooms. The sumptuous rooms, near the nursery on this floor. Make sure the baths are run and they have clean clothes. Give them their old servants and we'll meet in the hall soon to discuss matters of State."

"Thank you," Tevron said. "Sister."

Chapter Thirty-Three

The long green boat was rowed by two sturdy loyal Trolls, and Mindbender himself took the oars throughout the night as he secretly slipped across the sea to the Land of the Fairies. The Fairy Queen awaited him at the other side, having been alerted by the Harpster bird. The bird was too clever to reveal himself on the Troll's ledge, but had listened to the meeting in Mindbender's great hall, and reported to the Queen of Fairies all he had heard.

The boat glided into the pier at the end of the cobblestone walk that led to the Fairy's Palace. Mindbender stretched and put his magic boots onto firm land once again, relieved to do so, though Trolls like the water well enough.

"Hello, friend." The Queen welcomed him into her inner room with sweet smiles. She held in her hand her wand, which sparkled with stars. "You want more land for the Picts and Trolls, and you want the Palace, too. You want the humans gone. Where will they go?"

"My people would like to see them dead," Mindbender replied. "There will always be wars as long as there are humans."

"That may be true," replied the Queen, "but they are here, and as I said myself two nights ago, you are all of human stock. I told you that, my friend, and you wouldn't believe me, neither will your people believe it."

"I've read the old books," Mindbender admitted. "I know it may be true."

"It's an indigestible fact, sweet Troll. We Fairies have been here since the beginning of Minth, the planet you call Draxxt. We remember. We try to stay out of the way. But this is the start of perhaps yet another civil war, and we can't allow it."

"I'm going to enable my people to war," agreed Mindbender. "It's what they want, and it's the only way to peace."

"That's nonsensical. Peace doesn't come by war. Or not in this case, with a war that's gone on for centuries. I'm going to visit the Gracklen Palace and try to get this straightened out. Only the King and his brother, and their wives, can hold any hope for us now."

"Or you," Mindbender said, bowing his great head. "I came here to hope for some help from you and your Elves."

He stood up then, in the smaller confines of the Fairy Palace, and spread his arms. "I can tear this palace apart. I demand that you help me."

"No, you won't get any help from us," the Queen replied. "If anything, I will turn you all into toads." And she brought her magic wand down smartly on Mindbender's green head. He changed instantly into a small green toad, hopped to the door, chirped, and was eaten by the bird.

The Fairy Queen called her Elves to her, and the beautiful Fairies who danced in the clearing on a moonlit night. "Our time for celebrating and rejoicing is over for now. I will go to the human palace and I need your help. I have a gift for the child, and it must be delivered tomorrow. The Trolls and Picts are restless, and war is imminent. The prophecy must be fulfilled."

She set sail to Gracklen that night, with three other Fairies and two sturdy Elves. They put their feet on barren land, which sprouted spring flowers in their wake. Tripped lightly they did, over the verdant lands of the kingdom, flew past the Armgado Mines and over the Marlbrex Cliffs until the next evening they came to the valley beneath the King's gate. Under four bright moons, she summoned the healers in the glen, who gathered and bowed. As head of the coven, Ericaania was with the healers. She strode toward the fairy with arms outstretched.

"Ericaania."

"Merrywether."

They hugged, the Fairy surrounded by her maids in waiting, all webbed singing wings and gauzy silver gowns, and the Elves in green and brown buckskin. Ericaania bowed again and swept her arms toward the Palace. "You're welcome," she said. "Would you like something to eat and drink? Although I know Fairies drink only nectar and eat only berries and flowers, and

Elves eat succulent roots and drink mead. We have nothing that exotic to offer you, my Fairy Queen, but we'll do our best. The chefs in the Palace are quite inventive, though used to local fare."

"Thank you," the Fairy Queen whispered, blowing a kiss toward the Palace. The three maids with her, Fairies all, laughed like little tinkling silver bells in the glen and spread out over the clearing, touching their wands to each shrub and leaf, lighting the way with tiny fairy lights. They set their Queen's gift to the child on a hill of flowers near enough to carry it to the Palace when their Queen decided. The two sturdy Elves sat on a moss bank and contemplated the healers. Gathered in a bunch outside their building, the witches sang of joy and welcome. In the clearing to one side, there were dragons, huge sleek beasts with jeweled eyes and glittering scales in the moonlight. Amongst them was Faerydust, Lockjaw, and Fire-Smasher.

"How is our Moonraker and his whelp?" Faerydust roared, then lowered her great voice and turned a dusky shade of red. "He's been gone many moon cycles to Fairyland, with his partner from your shores, and we hear he's fathered a fine strapping young hatchling, who lives in the back of your palace with the monks to instruct him, madam."

The Fairy Queen glowed and touched her wand to a nearby shrub, which burst into light. "Yes, and they've named their hatchling Little Hakor, after your former king."

"An honor to His Majesty," rumbled Faerydust and snorted rainbows. Lockjaw moved closer to his mate, grooming her great neck with his steely teeth.

Ericaania ducked her head and smiled. "This is a great honor to our kingdom, Merrywether, to have you here with your entourage. But why have you come to these shores, after so long an absence?"

"The Planet of Minth is in danger, Queen Mother." The three Fairies with her fluttered and cried out with voices like moonlight on a summer breeze.

Ericaania waved her gloved white hand. "It isn't Minth, that fairy story, but our planet's name is Draxxt. Has been since humans first set foot in Gracklen, and it will remain Draxxt."

The Fairy Queen ignored her. She addressed the coven of healers. "We sent our herbs of peace to waft throughout Gracklen and the outback, but it seems that you are intent on subduing the Trolls and Picts, and the Fairies, too."

"If we must."

"Never will your kind of peace reign in human territory."

"You would have war forever?" asked the Fairy. She bowed her head and the lights in the glen grew dim. The four moons sailed behind a cloud and they were in darkness momentarily, until the Fairies lifted their heads and began to sing.

"There's a strangeness in the air," admitted Ericaania. "Here, my daughter-in-law is pregnant and there's rejoicing in the castle. Why don't you come and see her, Merrywether, and give her your blessing? It would mean much to the new Queen."

The Fairy Queen's wings were a silver blur as the first of the four moons peeked out from behind the mist. "The strangeness is wafted here across the valley from the outback, and I know it heralds a major change for the children of man."

The tips of her toes hovered above the green glen, then she and her three attendants lifted together the baby's gift, left the Elves and healers by the great building, and soared into the air above the Palace. The Queen Mother was left to saddle her dragon and follow.

Chapter Thirty-Four

Queen Almere felt tired. Her husband's menservants tended to his wounds, brought on by the tempestuous display of arms and strength with his half-brother two days before. She lounged in the nursery, her favorite room to relax nowadays, decorated with fey tapestries and childish paintings, an exquisitely carved cradle, and the little yellow flowered coverlet with lace that Mariette had sewn with her own hands, the first of many gifts for the coming child. A boy or girl? The room next to the nursery was filled with boxes and clothing of all description, lace and cream, yellow, blue and green, even pink in case the baby was a little princess in waiting. There were gold coins and sparkling gems from the Dragon's Hall, silver and ebony carved toys, little dolls from the far regions of the kingdom, and, of course, Ericaania's porcelain playthings from beyond the Agave Sea, and the tiny toy swords that Stannock had whittled for a son.

Littered with white sheepskin and goatskin rugs, silken carpets woven in the valleys beyond, and precious jeweled tiles, the floor was an expanse of color accented with the snowiest white to suit a young prince or princess.

Almere placed her hand on her belly where her baby stirred beneath her touch. Stannock, standing nearby, touched his wife on the shoulder. She winced as she saw the large wound on his arm.

"Why did you fight? It was so foolish," she said.

"He was a worthy opponent," Stannock replied. "One I am proud to call my brother."

The four Fairies slipped on a beam of moonlight through the portal of the Palace, into the nursery, with Ericaania, Stannock, and Almere in an enchanted circle, awaiting their gift. The Fairy Queen touched with her wand the wonderfully carven chest, small, about the size of a young hatchling newly born, and the Fairies set it down in a corner of the room. They stood back.

"A small gift, insignificant really, to be opened at the coronation of the child," Merrywether said.

"The box is beautiful," Almere said. "It's magically carven. What do all those symbols mean?"

"Yes." The Fairy Queen touched the chest with her wand and rainbows danced across the top and sides. A blue light emerged from behind the keyhole. "The symbols are a blessing for long life and great joy, a long reign of peace in the land for all, good health, and an honorable death at the end."

"Thank you," Almere said and Stannock echoed her. "Our child will treasure it forever, a gift from the Fairies who live across the Agave Sea. We'll tell her or him of your visit, and your kind words; and your blessing, I know, is on us, too, Madam."

The Fairy Queen reached into a cavernous billowing pocket of her gown and brought forth a golden key. She placed it in Stannock's hand.

"Keep this and open the chest when the baby is ready to reign, at the end of eighteen seasons, my dear, and this is a gift for you." She touched his wounds with her wand and the ugly redness drew together, became white, and closed to reveal new skin and no scars where Tevron's sword had pierced his arm and leg. His strained face became peaceful and soft, and he held out his hand in front of him.

"My lady," Stannock said. "I don't know what to say. You have also the blessing of my kingdom on you and your court."

"I know that," the Fairy Queen laughed, again like little tinkling bells in the beautiful room, where Almere rested beside her husband, and Ericaania rocked the empty cradle.

"There's unrest in the settlements," Stannock said. "We need help."

"Yes, I know that, too. The sweet scent of peace throughout the land is not enough. The Old Religion speaks of love and tolerance but that is not enough. Something must be done, my dears. The Trolls must return to their land across the sea, and the Picts with them. Only then will your kingdom be safe."

"That's what the wars were about," Stannock said. "It didn't work. We won the battle but apparently lost the war. They advance onto our lands and what we gave them isn't enough. It will never be enough for Mindbender and his gang of thugs until they have the Palace, too."

"I wouldn't worry about Mindbender," the Fairy said. Her maids tittered amongst themselves behind their silken hands. Their gauzy wings fluttered and they hovered above the cold tiles. "He's taken care of. Now we have to worry about the Picts and the mob of Trolls that he's left behind."

Stannock flexed his newly healed biceps, smooth and muscular. "Tevron was in charge of that."

"He failed, obviously. Making friends with the great Troll was a mistake. Where is he now, and his good wife?"

"They're on their way back to the settlements, with an army of dragons to relocate the children and their helpers," Almere replied, patting her belly and arranging a shawl about her shoulders. A cool breeze blew through the open portals of the castle and stirred the wild black curls on her head. "We've struck a bargain with him, to rule alongside his brother so that both brothers rule in the place of the old King Hakor, and Mariette will take her place as Duchess of Gracklen. A show of force like that might entice the Trolls and Picts to think again about invading Gracklen and the Palace. Our armies are ready, our dragons restless."

"You speak of war again," the Fairy Queen said, and her light dimmed once more, as though the moons had been covered by mist. "Perhaps the baby will be the answer."

"We must all unite or perish together," Stannock agreed. "But how?"

Almere twisted the moonstone bracelet on her slender tanned wrist. "It may be up to the next generation, not to us who have ruined so much of what could have been beautiful The child will be welcome. We'll fly a blue flag from the balcony of the Palace to announce a boy, and a red flag for a girl."

"Yes," the Fairy said. "There is a prophecy, as well. It may come to it, that magic will save us all."

"Or science," Stannock said. "Like in the ancient texts."

"We are stuff of legends," agreed Ericaania. Loud thumping on a lower floor interrupted them.

"It's Hakor," explained Ericaania. "He grows restless."

Chapter Thirty-Five

Jon remembered how it was sixty years ago, when he and Hakor were young men. The cycles of the seasons had piled up so quickly, so inexorably, and now Jon was left tending a weak old king who couldn't remember his name, and whose heart was tissue paper. Jon remembered the good old King Malcoom, who ruled with Hakor briefly as co-husband of their old Queen, and who sired the difficult and dour Tevron, so different from his father, so like Hakor except in looks. He remembered the two princes being born, the celebrations, and the murder of Malcoom. He wondered how much King Hakor remembered in the subterranean recesses of his mind, things that could never be erased. Sometimes music brought his charge back to reality for as long as the song lasted and Hakor hummed along, sometimes singing in his still rich but cracked voice of bygone eras, loves and wars. His wife visited daily but Hakor showed no sign of recognizing her.

"Sire, your midday soup and ale," Jon murmured, hobbling to his master's bedside. His form no longer recognizable as the vibrant man he once was, Hakor was confined mostly to bed. Too feeble to lift the old man anymore, Jon required help from younger male servants to bathe and dress Hakor. The old king's beard was white, his eyes still piercing.

"Who are you? What am I doing here, in this godforsaken room?" Hakor rumbled. "I want out." He tried to rouse himself from bed, and threw one massive leg over the side. Jon applied the restraints with the help of a young manservant. The King roared. "Who are you? Get out of here!"

The young manservant glanced at Jon, thinking, *they are both old men and should be dead by now. How much longer is this going on?* Outwardly, he brought a comb from the bedside table and began to groom the old man's hoary head of wild hair, which brought about a string of curses. The young man sighed, rolled his eyes, and left the room. *I don't get paid for this nonsense. Let old Jon handle the old man. I'm outta here.* His insolence was not unnoticed, but there was nothing Jon could do about it.

I can't stand this anymore. I'm too old to care for his Majesty, and his Majesty is suffering. It's time to put my plan into place. No one would blame me, least of all the King.

Jon wiped tears from his rheumy yellow eyes. It had been a good life, overall. The old king and Queen Ericaania had rescued him from poverty in the valley, taught him the Palace protocol, and placed him as a boy page in charge of the King's bath. The King had been robust and hearty, and Ericaania beautiful as she still was. As Jon matured, he had been given more responsibility in the Palace. They even brought his parents and brothers to live in the Palace, too, until the ongoing Troll Wars had martyred his brothers as heroes in the battlefield. Jon was too young at the time to join the army nor have a dragon of his own. He knew he would rejoin his brothers some day in the fields of Heaven, and they would all be young again, striding through the flowered meadows with sword in hand, hunting beast and singing the old songs. His parents had died of heartbreak soon after his brothers were slaughtered by the Trolls.

I've been King Hakor's son in spirit ever since. Jon spooned the broth into his monarch's mouth. He sat on the side of the bed while Hakor strained at his restraints. Chunks of boiled beast and root vegetables caught in his beard. The old man slurped at the soup. Jon offered the ale.

Jon had a secret. The old man was too good for poison, too hale, too full of fond memories. No, he would use the knife.

It was a fitting end to an old monarch who didn't deserve to wither away in obscurity and his dotage like this. Jon couldn't stand it anymore.

He cleared away the dishes and washed Hakor's face and beard, settled him in bed, as the old man clawed at him. "Who are you?"

"I am your friend, Jon, your manservant, sire. I'm here to look after you." Jon snatched the long hunting knife hidden in his cloak and hovered the blade above the old king. "God bless you, sire," he said, and the knife prepared to descend. Hakor's eyes flew open and he knew, Jon realized, what was to happen.

"Jon!" the old king cried, and Jon tensed his withered biceps to bring the knife into his king's still beating heart.

Hakor's head slumped and he groaned then was still. His breath no longer heaved the bedclothes up and down, his eyes rolled into the back of his head and there was a great rattle in his throat. Then the room was absolutely silent. The knife remained in Jon's hand. Tears ran down Jon's face so he could barely see, but he knew his king was dead.

He'd been spared the final ignominy of dispatching his king. A heart attack claimed him at the end.

The knife clattered on the hard tiles of the floor. Jon reached down, kneeling on arthritic joints, and plunged his own heart into the upward blade of the knife.

"My k-k-king!" he cried and was still. His blood ran over the tiles and onto a white rug nearby. A bird sang at the window, oblivious to Death. The three suns blazed through the portals onto a patch of floor and illuminated the white old man and his faithful servant on the floor. Jon's hand, spattered with blood, reached up to clasp his monarch's hand. That's how the young manservant found them when he came in to clear away the bowls.

"It was his heart," the doctor said. "His manservant, in his grief, apparently killed himself."

"It's over." Ericaania breathed an obvious sigh of relief. "My husband is dead."

"My father has been dead for many years. He just refused to give up," Stannock said, and they all put on the mourning colors. "It's an end of an era."

"We'll bury him with full honors due to a king," Ericaania stated. "Jon by his side."

So, the news was dispatched to the whole kingdom, which went into mourning for the obligatory ten sun cycles, at Stannock's request. The Queen Mother wore long black robes and a veil and refused to sob at the State funeral. Stannock and Tevron, too, were stony-faced. Mariette cried. Almere did not attend and was excused, as her time was very near and standing proved uncomfortable.

The citizens, who had more or less forgotten their indisposed monarch, gossiped suspiciously about the manner of his death. That was put to rest by the doctor's report, who listed the cause of death as heart attack. Jon's suicide went unreported and generally unnoticed, except by the coterie of Palace servants who knew him well.

"Hakor was never a good man," Ericaania admitted. "But he was loved dearly by his manservant, Jon."

"You visited him daily, Mother," Stannock said. "He will be remembered as a great king and good husband. We'll be sure the books list him as the end of the great monarchs of Gracklen, and he who continued to sire a line of kings unbroken from the beginning of time."

"His legacy will be duly noted," the court scribes promised.

"He's buried with Malcoom, my first and only love," Ericaania said. "A fitting burial. I want Jon buried at his feet, with a suitable stone. Jon's long life and loyalty must be duly noted."

"Done," the scribes acknowledged and began to write.

Chapter Thirty-Six

The Harpster bird regurgitated the toad into the Agave Sea. It swam through the swirling waters for many sun cycles, then came ashore on the other side, near the old castles and buildings of the Picts and Trolls which had been abandoned.

Ribbit. It hopped onto the shore. The bird flew back to its mistress, the Fairy Queen. She gave orders and her wand reached its magic across the waters to the shore of the old Troll country.

Be done, she whispered from her perch on the old green boat, and the toad – poof! Changed back into a large green Troll, who sat with its head in its hands and forgot all that had happened. Around Mindbender was only decay of old buildings and villages, old gardens and orchards, that had been long abandoned in the search for more land and better land, and an avarice which reached across the sea to designs on the Palace itself. But Mindbender didn't remember any of this.

He wandered many a day through the ruins, eating fruit and berries, and drinking spring water. He grew stronger, but his mind remained that of a child. A black bird was his constant companion, and over the sea to the south, the Fairy Queen received reports of her former friend, blundering through the ruined orchards of his prior home. Those reports made their way to Many Waters and Peace River, the settlements, and the Trolls and Picts he had left behind.

"Is it true?" a blue painted warrior asked. "Has our leader been enchanted and lost his mind?"

"They say it's true. Scouts have been to the old country and found him wandering, mumbling to himself, and unable to lead."

"What will we do?"

"Why, we must select a new leader."

"But who?"

The same Pict stood on a table and shouted for order. "Our former advisor is now a king.

He's promised us peace in exchange for a lasting truce. What should we do?"

"We all know about him." Scabbed and sore, an old Troll who had survived the wars waved his shield and sword into the murky air of their hall. "He can't be trusted."

"It was Mindbender who couldn't be trusted," replied another Pict. "We Picts have been under the thumb of the Trolls for too long. We could have had peace. We could have stayed in our own country, at the other side of the river, and been happy and well-fed."

"Who says we'd be happy under the thumb of the Palace of Gracklen?" A gigantic Troll pounded his green fist on the planks of the table.

Rattling the rafters of the great hall, a cacophony began, the Trolls against the Picts. "Yes – down with the Kings of Gracklen! Up the Trolls! Picts be damned!"

"Trolls are warmongers! Leave us to our peaceful ways, tending orchards and hunting. We were happy until the Trolls began to push their weight around."

"A great weight it is!" The Picts agreed, and the Trolls were pushed from the great hall by the sheer mass of painted blue bodies and poison-tipped spears.

Someone roared. "Wait!"

Except for a few exclamations, the room grew silent. The Trolls stood outside and bowed their heads. The Picts stopped pushing. Mindbender stood before them, ten cubits high, and the Fairy Queen beside him. On his shoulder peeped a small black bird with a purple chest.

Chapter Thirty-Seven

"I've been to Death and beyond," Mindbender shouted, "and know what it is to have a true friend." He indicated the Fairy Queen, who smiled and leaned on her sparkling wand. "There is a new day in the kingdom. The old king is dead. Long live the two Kings!"

"Down with the Kings!" chorused the Trolls, but the Picts glared at them and they were silent. They rubbed their wounds, still fresh from the recent wars.

"Do you want to lose your home and families for good? Then keep on fighting. Your attitude is not that of warriors, but of weaklings, who want something for nothing. If it's true that we're the result of an experiment, and we began as human, then we can say that we are improved on humans. What say you? We're an improvement."

"Yes!" The Trolls and Picts cheered.

"Then the human gene for discord can be weaned out of our bodies. We're not the product of evolution through many centuries, that have brought about someone like King Hakor to rule over us. We can rule ourselves! We have land, we have this fertile land that was given to us here in Many Waters, and we have our original land across the sea, which requires farmers and planters and hunters to tend. Why must we waste our time with war, running ourselves down?"

"No, we must not do that!" the Trolls shouted. The Picts all nodded and sat down.

"I've just come back from the Old Lands, and there are castles, buildings, orchards, forests, that we were too lazy to tend and so let get into disrepair. We preferred war. And whose fault was that?"

"Yours!" they all roared. The Trolls streamed back into the great hall and pounded on the tables. "Take back our old land! Tend the land! We don't need no handouts."

"Right?" Mindbender asked. His head glowed and elfin sparkles of silver ran down his body. Merrywether's translucent wings whirred in the still air, lending breath and credence to Mindbender's words.

"Right! It's your fault!"

Mindbender put one huge boot on a bench and stood with his mighty spear in front of him.

"I admit it. I am fate. I led you astray. But I've learned better, friends, and I'm here to say, let's work with the new kings. There's a new era in our land. We don't have to be bound by our history."

"Not bound by history!" the Trolls yelled and the Picts nodded. "Apologize!" they roared and Mindbender bent his great head in agreement.

"I apologize," he said. "I was wrong."

"Kill him!" shouted a young Troll, brandishing his sword.

"No, he'll lead us to a better future. Peace!"

"Kill him!" So, they debated into the night until the Fairy Queen touched the beams of the hall with her wand, and light sparkled to life throughout the room.

"I mustn't interfere," she murmured to the great Troll and disappeared. The bird chirped from her shoulder then followed her home, across the sea, to the crystal Palace.

Her subjects awaited her to dance in the moonlight and forget their worries. As Fairies do.

Chapter Thirty-Eight

The orphans settled into their new home in the Royal Palace. They, too, awaited the birth of a new prince or princess, though all the kingdom was in mourning for King Hakor, at Stannock's request. Some stubborn settlers in Peace River refused to relocate. Tevron and Mariette enjoyed the luxury of their new suites. They oversaw the education and play of the children, especially Mariette, while Tevron was involved in matters of State.

"What's in the chest?" asked Mariette as she knit a green gown for the new heir. Almere, uncomfortable, lurched to her feet and took the tapestry off the box in the corner.

"Merrywether, the Fairy Queen, gave it to the child as a gift, to be opened on the child's coronation day eighteen seasons hence," Almere said. "We don't know what's in it."

"Aren't you curious?" Mariette dropped a stitch and pinched her lower lip with her upper teeth. "I would be mad with curiosity."

"In fact, you are," laughed Almere. "But no, Stannock has the key, and I think there would be a curse on us if we opened the gift before its time."

"Well, it's your child."

"Like an arrow from our bow, the child will be free of our expectations and control as he grows."

"How do you know it's going to be a boy?"

"The size of my belly," Almere said. "It has to be a sturdy boy, like the old king, like his father, Stannock."

"Maybe she's an Amazon," observed Mariette, "like in our ancient history from Earth. From those books you have." She continued to knit.

Almere went into labor a day later, in her snow-white bedroom with midwives in attendance, a birthing pool, and Stannock pacing outside the door, for husbands were not allowed in the birthing room. The Queen Mother and Fairy Queen fluttered beside her birthing chair while she groaned with impending deliverance. The midwives tittered and smiled as the time grew near, and the doctor paced outside the door with Stannock. They gave one another condolences and encouragement.

The dragons were all aware. Outside the open portal of a large window, her faithful Fire-Smasher watched, too. Every now and then another dragon would take his place, hovering on scarlet wings to witness this historic occasion.

Almere groaned but didn't scream as she pushed. Her waters broke and rushed out into the birthing pool, which welcomed her with its warm embrace, and the midwife in charge wiped the Queen's forehead with a cloth, then urged, "Push, your Majesty. Push. I see the crown of a little head."

Ericaania wiped away a few tears and gripped Almere's hand. "It's almost over," she murmured, and Merrywether smiled, fluttered above the silken rugs, and touched Almere's swollen belly with her wand. Suddenly, Almere groaned mightily and screamed as the baby's head broke into view. The baby emerged into the hands of the midwives, sank into the warm waters of the birthing pool, and the cord was quickly cut.

"It's a boy!" Ericaania pumped Almere's hands and kissed her. "I'm ecstatic! You did so well! A little prince! And beautiful, perfect! How are you? He's your first child, my dear. The labor was one of love and longing for these many months for an heir. We have an heir! Fly the blue flag from the Palace ramparts," she commanded.

Stannock rushed in to hold his son. "We'll christen you Malcoom the Second," he said, unsure how to grasp the squirming bundle.

"Yes," Almere whispered. "Malcoom."

Ericaania smiled. The midwives rushed to clean the afterbirth and take care of the new mother, who groaned anew.

"What's this?" asked Merrywether. The chief midwife looked up, surprised. Outside the window, the dragons gasped. "She's not finished!"

"It's twins!"

Almere screamed once more, then again, and a little red head emerged, dropped into the midwife's hands, and slithered into the birthing pool. Stannock held his son and gaped.

"It's a girl!"

The midwife's expert hands cut the cord and held the child. "But what is this?"

"Something's wrong."

The baby cried, then cooed and gurgled in the midwife's hands. She placed her on Almere's chest, a daughter with red scales, a soft tail, and Almere's face.

"A hybrid foundling," said the Fairy Queen. "A love child. Nothing's wrong."

Stannock wrapped the boy in swaddling clothes and handed him to his mother. "You look after him," he instructed, his face flustered. "I have a kingdom to run, darling, but we will raise our children together."

"What about my – our – your daughter?"

"I'll raise her as my own until the time comes for her to leave. We'll call her Dracaena, the dragoness with the woman's face, who will rule."

"No," the Fairy Queen corrected, taking the baby in her arms. "Her name is Hope."

Stannock considered. "Generally, the first-born of twins is the ruler. But here, the old law must be modified. They will rule together, and thus the prophecy will be fulfilled."

"Fly a red flag, too, from the Palace ramparts, to announce the birth of our daughter," Stannock continued. "Yes, her name is Hope, and our son's name is Malcoom, and this is the beginning of a new reign, with Peace for all."

Epilogue

Tevron rode astride the proud Azazel to the bad-land where the Trolls and Picts had summoned him. In his hand, he held the kings' pardon and apologies for the atrocities of war and the unrest since. His rucksack boasted the many papers concerned with transfer of lands, castles, seeds, servants, and dragons to the Old Land where the Trolls wished to relocate. Mindbender, in his realm, accepted his crown.

With Tevron were four drakes of prodigious strength and cunning, who had served the Palace well and fought bravely. They were ridden by half a dozen stalwart Palace servants, versed in agriculture and ancient lore, which would be useful to the Trolls in their Old Land. After all, the Picts could live off the land. They had always done so and were not happy with their Troll overlords. Stannock and Tevron agreed to grant the blue people the land of Many Waters, at some distance from their old allies. The human settlers would return to Peace River, those who cared to come back. They could work with the Picts, if they chose, to develop the countryside so it was more hospitable.

"Call yourselves pioneers," Tevron told the Trolls when he met with the three races together in the Trolls' great hall. "You're going out to carve a paradise from a wilderness. We'll supply any help you need, but you must do the work on your own. These six strong servants will assist your king, and you'll be a kingdom in your own right, in your old lands across the Agave Sea. The Fairies will be your neighbors."

He turned to the Picts. "You have your own land now, and can hunt and fish in the tributaries and streams of Many Waters to your hearts' ease. Don't ever look beyond your borders with greed. Sure, you've learned your lesson now. Your neighbors will be the human settlers, and your orphans also will be looked after. We'll all share our knowledge, but if you wish, a great wall may be built along the borders of Many Waters, and you can be left in peace."

"We don't need a wall," a young Pict said, the same one who started the uprising in the hall against the Trolls a few days ago. "My name is Crack. We don't need a dragon and we don't need a king. We've always been an independent race. Now the Old Religion has begun to sweep through our land, and many of us believe in the love of our neighbors, but also we won't beat our swords into plows just now. We're cautious, King Tevron, but grateful."

"Some of us are," commented another Pict. "Crack doesn't speak for all of us. We have chiefs, but our chief must listen to his people. We don't follow a king, nor do we follow a chief unless he's in agreement with the people's will."

"I see," Tevron said. "We've never begun to study Picts, nor even the philosophy of the Trolls. That's our disgrace, that we simply wanted to subdue you both."

A human settler spoke up. "I don't feel safe living next to these savages," she said. "Our men are farmers and ranchers and can't protect us if they start pouring across that border. I want a wall."

"No wall," decided Tevron. "But it'll be many seasons before you all feel comfortable together, and maybe never."

"Never," declared the settlers. "We remember the bloodshed only a season ago. We want our lands here in the fertile belt, but we don't want the Picts and Trolls as neighbors."

"Yet you've lived with them as neighbors since the battle was won by our new king," Tevron said. "There's been unrest, but no attacks. What do you expect from them now that there's a covenant of peace?"

"I guess we could give them a chance," a human settler grumbled. "Seems only fair." The rest murmured in agreement.

"For ourselves, we'll keep to ourselves," announced Crack. "We don't need any help with hunting and fishing. That's what we do best."

"My sons could use some tips how to hunt the badlands," commented a farmer. "We're busy with our crops this year, they're just coming in, and a good crop it proves to be, too. But I have brave and adventurous children, a daughter, too, strong and tall, who love to hunt with bow and crossbow. Could they maybe hunt the land with your children, Crack?"

The Picts smiled. "We're pleased you ask for our help. That's unusual in our history. But we might allow our children to be friends. I think it's too late for us older folks."

"No, it's not too late," the farmer countered. "Not for us. You've never hurt us, except the Palace armies from across the valleys. Our big problem is our own kings." He glared at Tevron, who glared back.

The Trolls gathered around Mindbender, their new king. "We know what to do," they said. "We always did. But we'll miss the Picts."

"You'll miss us taking orders from you," Crack accused. He flexed his fingers. His arrows slung across his slight blue shoulders. His bow rested on the table in front of him. Mindbender put a massive hand on the offending Troll's shoulder.

"They're right," he said. "We treated the Picts as we were treated by the humans." Tevron continued to glare. Mindbender glared back. The Trolls moved to one corner of the hall and the Picts gathered around them.

"I think we're agreed," Crack said. "The humans have been our enemy all along."

"They divided us to conquer," a Troll said.

Tevron looked at his fingers spread across the table. He shuffled the papers he held.

"Here it says you each have your own lands," he stated. "Signed by King Stannock and myself. Much of the difficulty was brought about by our old king, I admit. That's history now."

"The old king? Hakor? We hear he's dead."

Tevron frowned. "Yes, and a new heir has been born to a peaceful kingdom."

"We didn't hear that. A prince to take the place of your kings when the time comes?"

So, they heard of the royal twins, a son and daughter, and the royal ascension in eighteen seasons.

"You and Stannock are young. Will you want to secede in eighteen seasons?"

"If we don't, it will be up to the children entirely. We have plans to expand our kingdom peacefully. That will require family time, and people time, and we won't make the mistake of hanging onto power after infirmity has made it improbable."

"Like has been done."

"Like has been done," Tevron agreed. "But we won't talk of that. The old king is dead, you're right, and new heirs arise. The fragrance of peace still blows across our lands. Let's work together for it, that our children may not know war and poverty."

Mindbender raised his great hand. "I agree to uphold the statutes of my kingdom. We're working to put them into place right now. Too long have the Trolls been divided and misguided. Too long have we relied on the Picts to do our work for us. They've been as slaves, and we apologize. We'll make it right," he promised. "But the Picts, too, have been to blame, you know that, Crack. You've been an ignorant and weak race, dependent on us Trolls to defend you against your enemies and ours."

"We've fought bravely, too," another Pict said, scarred from the wars.

"Yes, we've all fought bravely, all three races, and the dragons, too. The battles were really decided by Fate," Mindbender said. "Which brings us to the question, do we sign the agreements and start a new life in the wilderness, our former home, and allow the Picts and human settlers to continue with theirs?"

"Yes!" They all shouted and Tevron explained the terms once more, so there would be no misunderstanding. Their leaders signed, then the populace also signed. For hours they stood in line, with their signatures or their marks on the papers before them, as they all received the kings' sealed deeds for their new lands and goods. The Trolls got three strong dragons and the Picts got one, a young drake who appeared eager to serve. Mindbender stood with his head bowed and his crown on the table in front of him, co-signing for his new kingdom.

Some of the human settlers who had moved away decided to return to Peace River, others stayed in the newer lands along the southeastern shores of the sea. There was fertile land in both areas.

"What about the dragons?" the settlers asked. "They've always been loyal to humans. Will they join the Trolls and Picts peacefully and be obedient?"

"Yes, of course," a gentle voice roared and all were startled as the fiery head of the red dragon poked through their doors. "Our leaders were consulted by the queens and kings of Gracklen themselves, a few sun cycles ago, and we have always agreed with the wishes of our leaders. Besides, we dragons are adventurous. Ask Moonraker, who fathered a whelp with a Fairy dragoness, and now lives with his new family in the Land of the Fairies. We'll welcome a new challenge. Believe us, it's a pleasure to serve the Trolls and Picts. We're never far from our human masters, and our dens at the Palace grow crowded. And almost dirty." He laughed, great snorts of fire, and withdrew his head. "Give us space, give us air, give us freedom. We'll be happy to carry you on our backs. It's a pleasure. It's what we were born for, adventure and change, and our leaders' marks are on the deeds, too, if you will notice. The great clawed talons of Lockjaw, who carries her Majesty herself, and those of Faerydust, my mother, made their marks on the scorched surface of the Dragon Stone, to promise our allegiance."

"That suits me," Mindbender said. He raised a bushy eyebrow at the Pict leader and the old farmer who had challenged him.

"Me, too," they both agreed. There was a general murmur of consensus throughout the room.

A handful of malcontents joined a few Picts and Trolls outside the hall. They stood in a small group arguing amongst themselves, and finally walked away, arms around one another's shoulders. They agreed that the Gracklen Palace was deceitful and unfair, and they must work together against it. Mindbender smiled. Change was indeed in the air. And cooperation.

Here, in the great hall of the four races, the future of Minth was decided. A small black bird with a purple chest peeped and flew away to the southeast. It sang as it flew.

Dear reader,

We hope you enjoyed reading *Engaging The Dragon*. Please take a moment to leave a review, even if it's a short one. Your opinion is important to us.

Discover more books by Kenna McKinnon at https://www.nextchapter.pub/authors/kenna-mckinnon

Want to know when one of our books is free or discounted? Join the newsletter at http://eepurl.com/bqqB3H

Best regards,
Kenna McKinnon and the Next Chapter Team

About The Author

Kenna McKinnon is the author of a quirky mystery starring a schizophrenic female, *Blood Sister*; *The Insanity Machine*, a memoir with co-author Austin Mardon, PhD, CM; *Timothy Hill and the Cloak of Power*; and the more recent novella, *Ascending*. Her books are available in eBook and print worldwide on Amazon, Smashwords, Barnes & Noble, and in selected local bookstores and public libraries.

Her interests / hobbies include fitness and health, volunteering, reading, writing, music, and walking. She lives in Edmonton, Canada. Her most memorable years were spent at the University of Alberta, where she graduated with Distinction with a degree in Anthropology. She has lived successfully with schizophrenia for many years and is a member of the Writers' Guild of Alberta and the Canadian Authors

Association. She has three children and three grandsons.

References

Her author's blog:
http://KennaMcKinnonAuthor.com/
Twitter:
http://www.twitter.com/KennaMcKinnon
LinkedIn:
http://www.linkedin.com/in/kennamckinnon

Lightning Source UK Ltd.
Milton Keynes UK
UKHW040039050521
383075UK00015B/98